The Pharmacist
&
Her Daughter

The Pharmacist & Her Daughter
BOULEVARD *editions*
London 2005

BOULEVARD *editions*
is an imprint of
THE *Erotic* Print Society
Email: eros@eroticprints.org
Web: www.eroticprints.org

ISBN: 1-904989-03-9

Printed and bound in Spain by Bookprint S.L., Barcelona

The Erotic Print Society is a publisher of fine art, photography and fiction
books and limited editions. To find out more please visit us on the web at
www.eroticprints.org or call us for a catalogue (UK only) on 0871 7110 134.

ESPARBEC
TRANSLATED BY VALERIE ORPEN

The Pharmacist

&

Her Daughter

EPS

CONTENTS

Foreword

E sparbec is a literary phenomenon. To elaborate on this, I will need to revert to certain arguments that I put forth in the long preface to *From the Infinite to Zero* (the fifth and final volume of the *Anthology of Erotic Literature*), which featured a number of extracts from conversations I had with Esparbec.

Georges Pailler, better known as Esparbec (I mistakenly ennobled him in the *Anthology* by calling him D'Esparbec – a sign of respect), has used a number of pseudonyms during his long career: John Jensen, Victoria Queen, Georges Péridol... What is noteworthy is his prolific output as well as his style. Taking those two aspects into consideration, the title of my Esparbec preface for the *Anthology* was 'The Last of the Pornographers'.

Indeed, Esparbec refuses to call himself a 'writer of erotica', a label he loathes rather, he simply asserts his position as a 'pornographer'. It is this pornographer who produced, either directly or indirectly, some 500 novels between 1987 and 2003. He has written about 100 novels, but also, in his role as series editor for the publisher Hachette (now called Hachette Média 1000), he has edited some 400 titles.

At first, Esparbec worked only with professional writers. He then went on to include a lot of amateurs in his teams. His work method was always rigorous:

"After a year," he claims, "I was able to publish manuscripts I'd received in the post once those writers had agreed to undergo training in writing skills. I gradually retained the best

of these amateur writers and formed a stable of about a dozen writers who had started out merely as readers. Later, that method became more sophisticated; we would rewrite texts that were not good enough to be published and we would share them between ourselves. Most of the time, three people would work on a book, sometimes four. Generally speaking, I work in the initial stages with the author, then in the final stages with the rewriter(s) when the author has reached his or her limits.

"Another possible source that we use is confessions and requests. Some readers send us long letters (some anonymous, some not) relating their sexual adventures or exposing their sexual preferences. Some of them even set out their requests for the sort of scenarios that they wish to read. When this material is rich, I use it to suggest plots to writers whose imaginations are faltering or whose fantasies seem close to those of a particular 'client'."

But these are general principles. What is crucial is the way in which Esparbec envisages the writing of these different novels:

"As for the style, which is close to the 'degree zero' championed by Barthes, it mustn't form a barrier between what is told (or shown) and the reader. The style must aim to be transparent: the reader's gaze must see through it without noticing it like a voyeur looking through a two-way mirror. This neutral and behaviourist writing style refuses to use the 'specialised' vocabulary much in favour in the 1970s and 1980s (including a number of invented terms such as 'flaccide', which doesn't exist in French) or the porn vocabulary found in sex shops (which is currently being revived by certain female writers in so-called scandalous stories). Worse still are metaphors and

other figures of speech such as tropes, flourishes, witticisms and narcissistic embellishments. If the reader notices that a book is 'well written', then it's a failure; the reader is no longer visualising, he or she is reading. All my beginners are tempted to prettify their writing, to use a florid or self-conscious style, and I have to wean them off it. Porn writers must step aside in favour of their subject matter."

However, let us not be fooled. This writing style, which, on the face of it, seems so simple and direct, and which could almost be called primitive, is powerfully erotic. It is the result of an extreme form of control in the art of 'licentious' expression. Esparbec has turned his back on the ubiquitous pseudo-artistic pyrotechnics of contemporary novels, and prefers to focus, for his and our pleasure, on what we could call pure pornography.

And why shouldn't pornography cleansed of 'literature' (in the vulgar sense of the term) become real literature?

As he explains very clearly in his Postscript (a must-read, brimming with common sense), "There are good thrillers, good sci-fi novels, so why shouldn't there be good porn novels? Why should the writing of pornography be left to second-rate writers devoid of talent? Why should it end up in the dustbin of literature, in sex shops?"

That is why, my dear Esparbec, *The Pharmacist and Her Daughter* has been included in this series.

And may there be many others.

Jean-Jacques Pauvert

CHAPTER ONE: BÉBÉ SUCKS OFF HER COUSIN

Bébé would subsequently replay the whole scene over and over in her head, as if it were a film. She would see herself on her knees, in the kitchen, with her cousin Jéréme's big stiff cock rammed into her mouth, feeling that deep tremor which heralds a boy's imminent ejaculation. Jéréme, whom she could see from below, had that stupid look that boys have when they're about to come. His eyes were popping out of his head and his mouth was open. Just when his semen was spurting and hit the roof of her mouth, she heard the door creak. It couldn't be her brother because she knew that he was on the look-out in the garden. The hairs on her forearms bristled but it was too late for her to back away.

Her stupid cousin had seen and heard nothing. Like a laughable puppet, he was juddering from the spasms of pleasure at each spurt of semen. But she, Bertrande, she could see, and she did see. Behind Jéréme, Bob, her step-father, the second husband of her silly bitch of a mother, was standing stock-still on the kitchen threshold and, flabbergasted, was staring at her! She just had time to think, as she swallowed the last spurt, "God, what a bright idea of mine it was to suck off this idiot! I've really done it now!"

It was as if time had stopped and, instead of making a big fuss as she would have expected and alerting her mother who wouldn't have been far behind, Bob began to smile. Coldly. Cruelly. And her blood froze.

An hour earlier, she had been in her bedroom poring over her maths book. As soon as she had heard Jéréme arrive, she had had a fair idea of his intentions. It was always the same old story when her cousins, or her brother's mates, knew that she was home alone and that neither her mother nor her step-father would disturb them. She had been spot-on. Jéréme had not been in Bertrand's room for more than ten minutes when the boys came knocking on her door. They had entered without waiting for her permission, and as usual before 'it' began, they had started to snigger stupidly whilst nudging each other.

"Now what? Get lost, Bertrand! I've got to revise for my maths test. Go away! Take that idiot Jéréme into your room and leave me to get on with my work!"

"Oh, go on!" her brother had retorted, "just for a couple of minutes. It's Jéréme who..."

"That's a lie!" Jéréme had protested. "It was your brother's idea..."

"Don't listen to him!"

It was always the same bullshit. Flushed and bright-eyed, they'd laugh like drains. It wasn't exactly difficult to guess what they wanted.

"Oh, go on! He just wants you to suck him off a bit," her brother had managed to utter. "Be nice to him, Bébé. And I'll watch you. I like to watch you sucking off my mates!"

"No, leave me alone!" cried Bébé. "That's all you think about! And anyway, we don't have time. Mum'll be back any minute now with Bob. Go away, both of you!"

"Oh, go on, just a bit," Bertrand had insisted.

"Just the head!" had added their cousin, laughing. And they fell about again, like two morons; they were crying with laughter. Boys of that age could be such prats. Together, they

had unzipped their flies and arched their backs to show her their stiff pricks. Bébé had stamped her foot under her desk and pouted.

"No, I don't want to! Put them away! Stop mucking about, I'm not at your beck and call."

"Look at Jéréme's big hairy balls, don't you fancy bouncing them around in your hand while you suck him off?"

Jéréme had scooped his balls out to show them off to his cousin. They both felt she was on the verge of relenting. When her voice became whiny and a little bit tearful, it usually meant that she was about to give in. She'd been sucking them off for so long that those bastards could read her like a book.

"Show her your knob, Jéréme, you know that's what she likes best!"

Bertrand was the first to pull back his foreskin to reveal the pink flesh of his small, olive-shaped glans. Jéréme had followed suit, baring a fat lilac-coloured squashed plum.

"You're both gross!" Bébé had whimpered. "I hate you both! You're a couple of bastards! I'm not in the mood anyway! I only want to do it when I feel like it. So leave me alone and go away."

"Listen," had compromised Bertrand, "if you're scared of Mum, I don't mind being on the look-out in the garden. That way, you can suck him off in peace and when you're done with him, he can take over in the garden and you can suck me off."

"And what if Mum arrives while... How will we know if..." Blushing, she had stopped short. Jéréme could feel that she was weakening and had stood against the table and had put his big stiff prick with its retracted foreskin under her nose above her maths book. She could smell the sickly odour of the

head. He was so turned on that there was already a glistening dribble welling up from the little red hole at the tip.

"Well, why don't we go down to the kitchen?" had suggested Bertrand, who was never short of ideas when it came to nookie. "If I hear the car, I'll come and warn you and Jéréme can go home by jumping through the hedge."

She knew that it was possible. Her mother's 2CV made a terrible racket; you could hear it a mile away. In the time that it would take her to park, Jéréme, who lived next door, could rush home without being seen by going through the kitchen window at the back of the house.

She understood that they would not relent, and despite the fact that she had a bad feeling about the whole thing, Bébé had finally given in.

The boys had gone downstairs first; when she had arrived in the kitchen, Bertrand was already in the garden, on the look-out for the 2CV. Jéréme, sitting at the table, was pretending to read an old copy of *Paris-Match* that Bob had left lying around. Jéréme was always a lot more shy when he was alone with her than when there was another boy to mess around with.

She had put her hand on his shoulder and had pretended to look at the paper. Her heart was racing and she felt limp all over, as she always did before sex. She could see from his flushed expression that he wasn't feeling any more at ease than her.

"What are you reading? Is it interesting?"

"Well, it's an article on Madonna. You see... there's a photo of her..."

"Oh yeah. It's funny, Bob really likes Madonna; I think she's vulgar with her bottle-blonde hair. I think she looks like a slapper. What about you, Jéréme, don't you think she looks like a slapper?"

She had felt Jéréme's hand on her calf so she had leaned over his shoulder as if to read the article in question. His hand was gently edging its way up. She was pretending not to notice. Now his hand was on her thigh. Encouraged by her passivity, Jéréme, despite his shyness, began to caress her higher, getting insidiously closer to the humid warmth between her thighs. There was a lump in his throat. Suddenly her pubic hair tickled the back of his hand. His fingers had reached the top now, the spot where the skin was so soft, so warm, so moist, where the flesh divides, in the bush, on that moist and warm mouth hidden deep inside girls. His cousin was trembling. He had let his hand wander upwards and had become overwhelmed when he had realised that she wasn't wearing any knickers.

"Oh my God, you've taken them off!" he whispered. He grasped a buttock in his hand and caressed and fondled it. Bébé let herself be touched without reacting. She was quivering all over, as she did every time someone touched her bum. She could barely breathe.

"Oh God!" Jéréme had repeated.

"What? What did you say?"

He slid his folded fingers between her buttocks to touch the little wrinkled circle of her anus and pushed them further and finally sunk them deliciously into the hot and sticky slit. God, it was amazing how she could spread her legs, whereas other girls would always make a big fuss when you put your fingers there, but not Bébé; on the contrary, she would open up and all her flesh would be revealed, hot and moist.

"Can you feel that?" gasped Jéréme, still staring at the photo of Madonna. "I'm touching your... your clit and the... the..."

"Oh shut up!"

She had covered his mouth with her hand. His fingers were running up and down her sticky furrow and she started to tremble all over; it wasn't that he would frig her well, but as soon as anyone put their finger in her slit or groped her buttocks, it would happen! She just couldn't help herself. She took a deep breath. And suddenly, she came back to her senses and managed to back away.

"No! That's not what we agreed!" She knew that if he turned her on too much, she would be incapable of stopping him from doing whatever he wanted and she didn't want him to bugger her like yesterday. She was disgusted with herself afterwards because the boys would always make fun of her; when they pushed their cocks in her bum, it made her come so hard that she would scream her head off, and that would make those idiots laugh. It was only with her brother that she felt no disgust. They were twins, she and Bertrand; when he buggered her, it was as if she was doing it to herself, it wasn't the same.

Relieved to have been able to extricate herself from her cousin's fingers, she had felt like laughing when she had seen how crestfallen he looked.

"Right, enough pissing around, I've got to go back upstairs and revise my maths."

"Oh no, please. Look..."

To tempt her, he had shown her his big stiff penis with its revealed shiny glans.

"Oh all right, then. But I'll just suck you, OK, nothing else."

She had sighed, had knelt before him and had flicked her tongue over the red plum. Immediately, that damn greed of hers stirred deep inside her. God, how she loved it. She must have been abnormal to like sucking boys off so much. Other

girls were different. She was already soaked between her thighs and she felt hot all over. She gave him a second flick. They could hear Bertrand whistling in the garden.

"Don't you ever wash, you dirty boy? Your prick smells of cheese! Come here..."

She took his penis and led him to the sink. She liked to draw things out, to find a pretext to touch their penises for a bit longer. She let cold water run onto the glans then took a bar of carbolic soap and lathered it between her fingers. With the lather, she soaped her cousin's glans. She could feel him quiver under her touch.

Nevertheless, he didn't miss a trick. While she was pampering him, he was lifting her dress and leaning backwards to eye up her arse. She pretended not to notice. So he slid a finger between her buttocks.

"What are you doing? Stay still, how can I wash you if you keep fidgeting all the time? Jéréme, take your finger out of there, you naughty boy..."

"Just a finger, let me put my finger in..."

"You're such a pain!"

He knew what that whiny tone meant. Before she had time to change her mind as she had done earlier, he quickly squatted behind her. She placed her hands on the edge of the sink. He spread her buttocks. She felt his fingers touching her. They parted the hair, then one of them entered her bottom. She held her breath. She loved that so much, that filthy feeling, when a whole finger penetrated her. She heard him sigh.

"Jéréme," she whispered, "you like doing what we're doing, don't you? You like putting your finger in my bottom, don't you?"

"Yes... I love it... What about you?"

"Me too. We're disgusting, aren't we? If my mum knew the filth we get up to – she thinks I'm a little angel!"

He was twisting his finger so as to push it inside her while teasing her clit with his other hand. She was red hot and oozing. And suddenly, she felt a deep tremor within her which made her scream inwardly. She had come! But not fully. She had come, but she was still horny. She felt feverish, as if she was coming down with the 'flu.

"I'm going to suck you off now," she said in a voice that was still husky from pleasure, "and then I'll go and revise my maths."

"Let me put it in your arse," Jéréme had begged her. "I won't hurt you, I promise. Please, Bébé! I'll just put the end in..."

"No, you said that yesterday and you put it all in and then my arse was hurting all day. Your thing's bigger than my brother's."

Despite her horniness, she had not given in. She had quickly squatted in front of him. His glans smelled of soap. She took it in her mouth and gobbled it greedily.

"Oh, Bébé, Bébé," moaned Jéréme, "let me put it in your arse. I'll be gentle, I promise. Just the end..."

But she had stood her ground and had sucked him until he could no longer resist.

"Bébé, oh Bébé," sobbed Jéréme.

And so just as his come was spurting, her step-father appeared. Jéréme saw nothing. The door was behind him. There was a long silence. Then Bob's sickly smile.

"Well, well, I see we're having fun here. Your mother's going to be happy, Bébé, when she finds out how you're revising your maths!"

"Please don't tell her, Bob! He made me do it! Bob, don't tell Mum!"

She ran over to the sink to spit out the come and then ran the tap, under the mocking and evil gaze of her mother's husband. How smug he looked, the bastard! She hoped he wouldn't say anything to Mum. And why didn't Bertrand warn them? How come they didn't hear the 2CV?

"On yer bike, you little twat," said Bob to Jéréme, who was white as a sheet. In a flash, the cousin dived into the corridor.

Bob and Bébé were facing each other. Bébé, blushing, bowed her head. Bob smiled his funny smile and it carried on like this for a while. Finally, they heard the 2CV chugging into the drive, followed by the voices of the pharmacist and Bertrand in the garden. Why was Bob still silent? And suddenly, Bébé saw a man on the threshold. He had entered without making a sound, as if he had just popped up through the floorboards. He was slim, not to say skinny, and very pale, unhealthily pale, as if his face hadn't seen the sun for a long time. He too, like Bob, was silently contemplating Bébé. His yellow eyes were filled with burning lust. Who was he? How long had he been there? Had he seen her sucking off Jéréme? Bébé wanted the ground to swallow her up.

"Ernest," said Bob, "I'd like you to meet Bébé, my wife's daughter. Bébé, this is Ernest, my cousin. He's just out of prison. He'll stay with us tonight; tomorrow, your mother will drive him to your cousin's in Agen, the one whose husband is a lawyer. He deals with social rehabilitation. He's promised to find Ernest a job in the area."

"How do you do, miss," said Ernest politely. "Sorry to disturb you."

He touched his forehead with his fingertips in a gesture of

salute and grinned wanly.

"It's hard to find a job when you've got a police record!" he explained. "It's really sweet of your dear Mama to take care of it."

"It goes without saying," said Bob, "you're my cousin. We have to stick together as a family."

Bébé was relieved to realise that the newcomer had seen nothing. Bob and Ernest must have arrived ahead, in a taxi, or another car. That's why Bertrand couldn't warn her. Her mother must have been following them in the 2CV. That old banger was as slow as a wet weekend.

"Bob," pleaded Bébé in a whisper, out of earshot of the newcomer, and pulling her mother's husband by the sleeve, "you won't say anything, will you? Promise?"

"I'll think about it," said Bob, "we'll discuss it later... Right now, we have to take care of Ernest."

He stroked her cheek and she shuddered all over. This reaction of repulsion did not escape her step-father.

"Just you wait and see," he whispered, a split second before his wife came into the kitchen, pushing a shopping trolley filled to the brim with frozen food.

Chapter Two:
Bébé shows her knickers to step-daddy

As soon as Laura Desjardins had arrived, followed by her son who was pushing a second trolley, the whole house was in uproar owing to the unexpected visit of their guest. While they were busy emptying the trolleys and filling up the fridge and freezer, the children managed to exchange a few whispered words.

Bébé was bitterly reproaching her brother for what had happened and told him that Bob had caught her giving Jéréme a blow-job. Why had that idiot Bertrand not warned her? He explained that he hadn't been wary of the car that had stopped in front of the house and when Bob and his cousin had got out, it had been too late to warn them. Particularly since he had had to help Ernest with his luggage. He tried to reassure his sister; maybe Bob wouldn't say anything. Bébé wasn't so sure.

She knew that her step-father hated her. And she knew why. She remembered the way she had teased him that hot summer by wandering around with practically nothing on in his presence, as if he wasn't a grown man. She was certain he hadn't forgotten about that.

Their mother interrupted their private conversation and took her upstairs to the second floor where part of the attic had been converted into a guest bedroom. This bedroom was one of the favourite playrooms of Bébé, her brother's friends and her cousins. She had been buggered there countless times, kneeling on the narrow bed that squeaked horrendously. This was where the ex-con would spend his first night of freedom.

She helped her mother to make up the bed and tidy up, for when the room wasn't being used for guests, it served as a junk room. While they were bustling about, her mother was singing the praises of poor Ernest. It was a real sob story: an unhappy childhood, alcoholic parents, getting in with the wrong crowd, car thefts; it sounded like a bad soap opera to Bébé. Before returning downstairs to prepare dinner, they opened the window to let some air into the stuffy room.

~

Bébé didn't trust this Ernest bloke in the slightest. He was just a small-time crook who was getting a bit long in the tooth and his deathly pale skin made him look ill. What she hated most about him was his shifty look and his false humility typical of those who are supposedly 'hard-done-by'. Nor did she care for the honeyed tones he used when, pretending to be a reformed baddie, he described, with a tremor in his voice, how the prison chaplain had so kindly helped him back onto 'the straight and narrow'. While he rattled off this nonsense over dinner, the two siblings exchanged knowing glances; they were both stunned that their mother, who was far from stupid, could fall for this play-acting. Meanwhile, Bob looked as if he was trying very hard not to burst out laughing at his cousin's whining. But he also looked smug every time his mocking gaze met that of his step-daughter; she would blush to the roots of her hair and would hunch miserably over her plate.

When the conversation turned to the sort of job that Ernest could do, Bob spoke up to praise his cousin. According to him, Ernest was good with his hands and had very nimble fingers; even when he was young, he was the champion of picking

locks or opening a safe if you'd forgotten the combination. Moreover, he was terrific at starting a car if you'd lost the ignition key. He could also climb onto roofs and remove tiles without making a sound. He could do absolutely anything. The twins could tell that this ambiguous praise was making Ernest uncomfortable. He obviously preferred them discussing his Christian virtues than his burglar's credentials. But Laura did not notice any possible malice and naively suggested that he fix the washbasin in the guest bedroom – the U-bend had sprung a leak. Ernest seemed delighted to lend a hand and, as soon as he had finished eating, he went up to the second floor with his toolbag. He had his own toolkit that he kept locked with a combination lock and which he took everywhere with him. Curious to see him at work, Bertrand accompanied him to lend him a hand.

Thus, Bertrande unexpectedly found herself alone with Bob and her mother. She immediately felt panic-stricken in the pit of her stomach. Hopefully, Bob wouldn't use his cousin's absence as an opportunity to tell her mother everything. She cast him an imploring look and while her mother was putting the leftover cold meat back in the fridge, she grabbed his arm and pleaded with him again in hushed tones, "Please, Bob, I beg you! Don't tell her!"

"Give me a good reason why I shouldn't," he sniggered. "After all, she is your mother, she has to keep you on the straight and narrow."

"I'll do anything if you don't tell her."

"Anything? Really?" whispered Bob, stroking her hand. She pulled her hand away involuntarily, as if a snake had touched her. When she saw Bob purse his lips, she regretted her gesture, but it was too late. He got up, looking grumpy, and

went over to the sofa where he lay down with his paper. At that moment, her mother returned and Bébé helped her to clear the table. She knew that usually, her mother and Bob would stay downstairs and watch TV. He would almost certainly tell her everything as soon as they were alone. However, there was the slim chance that he wouldn't tell her tonight, because his cousin was here. Having fixed the washbasin, Ernest would probably come back down to keep his hosts company.

Bébé was worried sick and moping about; she couldn't decide whether to go to her room or not.

"You should put some music on," suggested her mother. "We'll have a liqueur with Ernest when he comes down again. Is that all right, Bob? It would be nice for the poor lad, don't you think? He must feel like a fish out of water..."

Bob, with his paper spread out on his lap, grunted his assent. Bébé approached the stereo and crouched to look for a CD in the rack. She had crouched without thinking and it was only when she saw Bob's paper move and him staring straight at her knees that she realised she was revealing her thighs. She hadn't done it on purpose, and the very idea that he could think otherwise made her flush angrily. Instinctively, she brought her knees together and pulled her dress over them. But, as earlier, when she had moved her hand away, she immediately regretted this reflex of modesty when she saw her step-father's smile harden.

"By the way, Laura," he said, staring mockingly at his step-daughter, "there's something I've really got to tell you. You're going to laugh..."

Bébé felt as if she'd been punched in the stomach; she felt a rush of blood to the head and without hesitating, she spread her legs as much as she could so that her dress rode up well

above her knees. From where he was lying, Bob couldn't miss her knickers. She avoided his gaze and pretended to rummage through the rack. But he was silent.

His intrigued wife asked him what he wanted to say. Trembling all over, Bébé looked at him. Partly hidden behind his paper, he was shamelessly ogling his step-daughter's crotch. His wife couldn't see what he was up to. She repeated her question.

"What did you want to tell me, Bob? Is it about your cousin?"

Her thighs wide apart, Bébé pleaded Bob with her eyes. He smiled feebly and cleared his throat.

"Oh, I forget," he said, "you know how it is, you think of something and then it's gone..."

Bébé thought about what he could see under her dress. She was wearing a tiny pair of knickers which were very narrow at the front; they penetrated her and cut her slit in two. She was sure he could see a lot of hair, as well as her labia bulging on either side of the fabric. As usual, every time she exhibited herself, she could feel her belly melt and her hands go clammy. She grabbed a CD at random and put it in the player. She was so overwhelmed that as she did so, she involuntarily closed her thighs a little.

"Yeah," said Bob, "I've forgotten, but I'm sure it'll come back to me."

She was immediately aware of her blunder and opened her thighs again. She had reacted so fast that her knickers had got wedged in her slit. From the corner of her eye, she saw Bob close his mouth and prop himself up on his elbow so as to get a better view. The music began.

It was Mozart. Despite the fact that Bébé had no reason to remain crouched by the stereo, she remained in that position

so as to disguise her lack of composure, as much to her mother as to Bob, so she pretended to choose other CDs for later. Bob's eyes were fixed on her crotch. The situation was clear. Ever since he had caught her with Jéréme, Bébé had known that there was only one way to buy his silence.

Now that she had made her decision, she realised that it had cost her less than she had expected. She slowly got up. Her head was spinning and her belly felt heavy as it always did in the anticipation of sex games, like a sort of feverish anticipation in her flesh. Her breasts felt heavier and her nipples tingled.

On top of everything else, she now had an overwhelming urge to pee. She had to go, but she also had to let Bob know that she would be back soon. How could she make him understand that she consented to his proposal? There was only one way.

"I'm going to the loo," she announced to the assembled company, "and then I'll spend a bit more time with you."

This seemed to astonish Laura. Normally, as soon as her daughter had gulped down her dessert, she would shut herself away in her room. But she told herself that Bébé was breaking her daily habit in honour of her husband and his cousin, and she was grateful to her for that.

CHAPTER THREE:
INCESTUOUS GAMES, CONJUGAL GAMES

I t was a running joke in the family that, as soon as the
evening meal was over, Bébé would yawn conspicuously
and go up to bed.

Her brother would make fun of her: "She's incredible, that
one! As soon as she's eaten, beddy-byes! Like a python!"

Naturally, he would take the mickey out of her so as to allay
suspicion. He knew why she was in such a hurry. His sister
liked to wait up for him to come and bid her 'goodnight'. And
this would inevitably lead to one of those sex games they had
enjoyed so much since their innocent childhood days.

When Bertrand entered her bedroom, his sister would always
pretend to be asleep. She would lie in a strange position, with
her face turned towards the wall and hidden behind her hair
and her thumb in her mouth; she would be on her back and,
under the covers, one could make out her knees which were
pulled up and spread wide.

Laughing up his sleeve, Bertrand would unzip his fly, or even
take off his trousers altogether. Then he would masturbate
to make his penis grow harder while he contemplated his
'sleeping' sister. When his prick was nice and stiff, with the
head exposed, he would tiptoe towards her.

"She's fast asleep," he would whisper, "and here was I,
wanting to give her a big goodnight kiss. Never mind... My
little sister didn't wait up for me, she's already asleep and
sucking her thumb."

He would lift up the sheet and the covers and fold them

back onto her feet. As if on purpose, his sister's nightie was hitched up over her tummy and because she was on her back with her legs wide apart, Bertrand could see her gaping cleft between the hairs.

"Ooh, the naughty girl, she's sleeping with her pussy open. She doesn't realise that her brother's looking at her. She should be ashamed of herself! You can see everything, even her arsehole... Ooh, the dirty little minx! I won't kiss her, just to punish her!"

Bébé would suck her thumb noisily and spread her legs even wider. The slit of her pussy was gaping even more, revealing the protruding inner labia and the clitoris.

"Well, fancy that," said Bertrand, "this bit is very red and wet. Has that little lech been playing with herself? It certainly looks like it, just from the smell! She's even made the sheet wet!"

He would brush the soaked hair around her slit with his fingertip. He could see his sister's belly quiver and hear her breathing stop. Her clit would impertinently become erect and a trickle of moisture would glisten in the hollow of her vulva.

"This naughty little wanker is sound asleep," Bertrand would whisper. "I'm sure she's been doing nothing but fiddle with herself while looking at magazines. That's why she's so tired."

Slowly, very slowly, his fingers inched their way through her hair, getting nearer to the pink moist flesh...

"I mustn't wake her," he murmured, as if he was talking to himself. "I'll take advantage of her being asleep to touch her crack without her realising. I'll open up her pussy and tickle her clit, just like she did. I like it when it's all sticky like that, it looks like a big fat mussel! It's her fault for sleeping with

her legs apart. Imagine if it was Bob who'd entered her room instead of me... He could do anything he liked to her, she'd still be fast asleep!"

He would continue to part her flesh, and finger her warm folds, freeing her clitoris and gently tapping it to make it grow. With her thumb in her mouth, Bébé would endeavour to breathe normally. From between her eyelashes, she could make out her brother's stiff 'willy', with its blatant red tip. Bertrand would bring his face closer to the sleeping girl's crotch and sniff the slit while he teased her with his fingers.

"Oh, isn't she naughty! She smells of wee, and her clit keeps getting bigger and bigger... It's all red, just like a little strawberry... I wonder what it tastes like..."

In order to find out, he would flick his tongue over the tiny mound of flesh. Oh, it was wonderful, it felt like a hot thunderbolt all through her body! Her heart would leap in her chest, her nipples would harden, a warm juice would start to ooze from between her legs like blood from a wound. Then, she knew what would follow, for after having coated his finger in this juice, her brother would insert it into her anus, and it would become so intense at that point that she would start to tremble. Then he would lift her by the hips and turn her over like a big, lifeless doll and she would allow herself to be shifted without waking up.

"I'll take advantage of the fact that she's still fast asleep to bugger her," muttered Bertrand. "I'll push my prick into her bottom and I'll shoot my load inside her."

Moving like a sleepwalker, as if he really was trying not to wake her, he would position her onto her stomach and would fold her legs under her so as to lift her behind.

"There! Her fat arse is nice and open, I can put it in now. If

she could only see herself, with all her bits on show! She really is a little slut!"

He would spread her legs and standing behind her, he would hold her hips and insert the head of his penis into her anus.

"There, it's in, all I have to do now is push." And he would push, making the hard rod of flesh penetrate the arse of his sister who was dribbling with joy into her pillow. Naturally, after a while, they would find it impossible to keep up this pretence and Bébé and her brother would collapse into hushed fits of laughter.

What made them laugh so hysterically was the thought that, just beneath them, their mother and Bob had absolutely no inkling of what they were up to. They thought they were two little angels!

Because they practically never went out like most other teenagers, their mother thought they were innocent kids.

"Oh God," whispered Bébé, arching her back to enable her brother's cock to penetrate her more deeply, "imagine, they're watching the telly thinking we're asleep!"

She could feel her brother's soft, warm balls, as downy as two peaches, knocking against her labia. She reached out beneath her to touch them.

"Stop it," grunted Bertrand, "don't do that, you'll make me shoot my load!"

Shoot. Bugger.

At any given opportunity, they would use the most obscene terms to describe their actions to each other.

"Oh no, don't shoot yet. Bugger me a bit longer. I love feeling your cock in my arse!" simpered Bébé, whose voice was wavering with pleasure.

But even though Laura Desjardins never imagined for a

moment the sort of fun her children were having, they would also have been astonished, not to say deeply shocked, to learn what was happening downstairs and the way their mother was behaving with her young husband.

Every evening, while she was watching TV with Bob, Laura Desjardins would melt as, after her son had bid them goodnight, she heard him go upstairs and politely knock on his sister's door to kiss her goodnight.

"Did you hear, Bob? He's gone up to say goodnight. He never forgets! Even when they've had a row. Isn't it sweet for a brother and sister to love each other that much? Especially at that awkward age!"

When Laura asked his opinion like this, Bob would wince. He didn't much care for his wife's offspring. But he played his cards close to his chest. He was living the life of Riley in this house and, like a lot of very young men who marry older women, his wife was like a second mother to him. One who earned a good living, who owned the biggest pharmacy in town, which allowed her to support him. Bob was a barman by trade but was nearly always unemployed because his wife didn't like him to work nights; at night, barmen are exposed to all sorts of temptations from 'women of easy virtue'; and after all, she hadn't remarried to end up sleeping in an empty bed. Thus she preferred him to stay at home since he refused to consider any other job. Besides, he made himself useful around the house, he didn't mind doing the housework or the shopping, and his wife didn't seem too bothered by the situation. After all, there were househusbands in countries

like Sweden, weren't there? Why should men have to go out to work? The pharmacy was doing well and Laura earned more than enough to pay the bills.

As for bone-idle Bob, he would 'force himself', as it were. He would shudder with horror at the recollection of the sleepless nights he had spent listening to drunks talking bollocks. Laura was admittedly no spring chicken but she was a terrific slut in the sack and Bob had always liked a bit of nookie. With her, he had met his match at last.

She was all the more of a 'slut' that it had come to her late in life, with Bob as it happened, who had 'discovered' her filthy side. Mind you, Laura had had to make up for lost time; her first husband, the twins' father, had not exactly been highly-sexed. What a difference when, after two years of widowhood, she had met Bob!

Since their marriage three years ago, she still couldn't get over the fact that a man could look after all her orifices so well. She consequently forgave him for occasionally becoming irritated when she displayed her fondness for her children. "He's jealous," she would think. And that would upset her a little, but she also felt flattered.

As soon as Bertrand had gone upstairs to his sister, it would start. Laura would grow languid and would snuggle up to Bob who would leap at the chance that they were rid of the brood to paw her in a rather vulgar way, which he liked to do outside the bedroom.

"Come now, Bob, stop it," simpered the pharmacist when he started to slide his hand under her skirt. "What if the children came down?"

"You know very well that they never do."

Blushing, she let her young husband (she was forty and he

was barely thirty and this age gap often gave her the deliciously incestuous feeling of sleeping with a teenage boy) undo her bra and remove her knickers. Sitting on the armchair in front of the television, she knew what would follow. Not what was on the box, of course, which she wasn't really watching. Once he had taken off her knickers and bra, Bob would lift up her skirt and unbutton her blouse. He didn't like women to be completely naked; he preferred her to be partially clothed, with those parts, and only those parts, which are normally hidden to be revealed and the other parts remaining clothed, precisely to highlight the indecent nudity of the exposed parts.

Laura obeyed her husband's wishes and never wore tights, only stockings and suspenders. Once he had bared her breasts and tucked up her skirt, Bob would resume his seat in front of her, next to the TV. Flushed with emotion, she pretended to be engrossed in the film while he looked at her. And he enjoyed what he saw very much.

This curvaceous forty-year-old with her handsome and serious face that was barely made up, with her hair scraped back into a severe bun, she sat there, in front of him, just for him, showing off her pussy and her big tits with their generous pink nipples. He had made her lift one leg up over the armrest so as to make her hairy slit gape, and because she was sitting on the edge of her seat, he could even glimpse her anus between her rounded buttocks.

Her cheeks were red and her eyes fixed on the television screen, for this beautiful and buxom pharmacist from Villeneuve-sur-Lot didn't dare look at her lout of a husband. It made her so horny to exhibit herself in this way that the juice was trickling between her hairs.

"Is that film interesting?" he asked her after a while.

"It's very good, honest, Bob," she would croak, "you should come and see for yourself... (she would modestly lower her voice at this point) instead of looking at this..."

"Well, you see, I disagree with you. I much prefer to look at your pussy and your tits than watch those crappy Yank soaps. I think this is a lot more fun. Right now, for instance, your crack's open as if it was hungry... and your clit's all hard, the little devil!"

"Keep your voice down!" whispered the pharmacist. "The children could hear you. And besides, Bob, you know I don't like it when you talk like that, it embarrasses me."

It was true that she was blushing, but she was also wet. He made no bones about it either.

"You're soaking! You should put a towel under you or you'll stain the armchair!"

"Bob!"

"Let me have a look, spread your legs so I can see your cunt. You know I like to see all your holes, especially when they're gaping like that."

She pouted in a mock contrite way but went along with her young spouse's demands. When he treated her like this, she had the impression, because of the age difference, that she was exhibiting herself to a bad boy, and this aroused memories of her distant adolescence. It was a good thing, she thought, that the twins weren't as mischievous as she had been at their age.

She lasciviously hooked her other leg over the other armrest because she knew that that was what Bob wanted. He loved it when she adopted that obscene position reminiscent of the gynaecologist's stirruped chair because it revealed 'the whole caboodle', and Bob, who was a bit of a voyeur, feasted his eyes on this improper sight that she offered him: first of all, in the

foreground, he could see her stilettos, which he forced her to wear, even around the house; then her slender ankles and her plump but shapely legs encased in black silk stockings; further up, he could see the white flesh of her thighs between the suspender straps. And finally, right at the top: the object of scandal, both hideous and magnificent, the tuft of shaggy hair, the big pink wet gash, the little bits of flesh sticking out, the red orifice of the vagina and the brown eye of the anus.

"I love it when you pose like a whore but your face still looks dignified."

Laura Desjardins pretended not to hear this ambiguous compliment but it titillated her nonetheless. She impatiently thought of the forthcoming attractions. Would he want her to give him a blow-job? Would he bugger her? Would he spank her (for he often spanked her naked bottom to punish her for exhibiting herself so indecently)? And afterwards, after reddening her buttocks, would he take her from the front, by way of a change? The pharmacist's heart was pounding wildly and she could feel her nipples hardening on her big breasts, of which she was a little ashamed; she called them her wet nurse's breasts. But Bob liked them, he enjoyed playing with them.

"Spread your pubes," he said, "I can't see your hole properly."

"Oh Bob, please! It's open enough!"

"Do as you're told. You're watching the telly, I have to have my fun too. Open your hole. I want to see it gape more than that! I want to see it dribble..."

She would open her vulva with both hands, crimson with shame and horniness. The towel which she had placed under her was getting damp from her juices. God, how this devil of a man made her wet!

"Now masturbate," said Bob, when he noticed that she was losing her head. It was always the same palaver. She was such a bloody hypocrite.

"No," simpered Laura, "you know I don't like doing that."

"Liar. Go on, masturbate a bit. Touch your clit and pinch your nipples at the same time."

Laura Desjardins breathlessly obeyed her perverse husband's commands. She would feel so ashamed when he demanded that she masturbate in front of him, but she couldn't deny that it turned her on so much that she sometimes made herself come right in front of him. She would feel offended afterwards when he made fun of her. But she knew that that was the price to pay so that he would finally attend to her needs.

When the time came, he would order her to get undressed. So that he didn't have to wait, she would remove her clothes as quickly as possible and would stand totally naked, but for her black stockings, in front of him. She would wait for his command and watch as he opened his fly and pulled out his stallion-like cock. If he said to her, "get on your knees, you whore", that meant that he wanted to come in her mouth, like with a prostitute. If he said, "turn around", then he would spank her to begin with before buggering her over the table.

So she would turn around to show him her arse and she would hear him snigger. He would mercilessly make all sorts of disagreeable remarks about her large rear. He would cruelly pinch her buttocks and pat them so as to make them jiggle about ludicrously.

"Look at that... Look at that fat arse. When you walk in the street, all the men turn round to ogle it! It's obscene, darling. It's the arse of a dirty slut!"

"Bob, please! Why do you say such things?"

"Bend over and spread your buttocks with your hands…"

Crimson-faced, Laura obeyed. Bob would laugh when he saw her anus enlarged like a wild boar's eye in the midst of the hair.

"If you could only see your arsehole and how open it is. You want me to bugger you, don't you? Own up!"

"Bob!"

He pouted in disgust. "You should be ashamed of yourself. You're a respectable woman, a pharmacist, a mother, and yet you show me your arse like that. What would your customers say if they could see you now? And your children? The poor little angels…"

"But it's you who's asking me to do this, Bob."

"That's not a good enough reason. An honest woman would refuse. But you're only too happy to oblige. You deserve to be punished."

He would go and sit in the armchair and it would be the best moment. Quivering, and feeling like a little girl about to be punished, she would lie down across his lap. He would reach under her and put his hand between her thighs and push his thumb into her vagina. Holding her thus, crushing her vagina, he would lift her up to force her to spread her buttocks and then he would spank her, as hard as possible, methodically. He would redden those cheeks, paying particular attention to her anal area. He loved to strike her directly on the anus while pinching the gooey flesh of her vulva between his thumb, which was still shoved into her vagina, and his fingers. At this stage, Laura would lose all modesty and would wriggle about comically, begging him huskily to hit her even harder.

"Harder, Bob, harder… Hurt me! Make it red! I want it to burn… Oh, don't stop, darling, don't stop, punish your big fat

slut! Oh, I love it so much... Oh yes, Bob, on the hole, on the crack... push your fingers in, aaarrrrghhhh, oh God, I'm going to scream, I'm going to scream, put your hand over my mouth, Bob, or I'll wake the kids!"

"I need both hands. Just bite your wrist."

He would spank her with all his might. And each slap would cause warm fluid to spurt between his fingers like a big juicy fruit.

When his arm ached and her arse was as red as a beetroot, Bob would stand her up again. He would gaze with satisfaction at his wife's face bathed in tears.

"Now that your arse is nice and hot, I'm going to bugger you, my darling."

"Oh yes, Bob, bugger me. You can do whatever you like to me."

Still sobbing and almost hysterical, she would lie face down on the table. Then, like Marlon Brando in *Last Tango in Paris*, Bob would take a knob of butter from the butter-dish on the table and would rub it onto his penis. Then he would pour himself a glass of wine and take a sip before positioning himself behind his wife who parted her buttocks with both hands to offer him her anus.

She could feel her heart pounding. Her bottom was burning and she could hear Bob savouring his wine. Then he would place the glass on her naked back and she would shudder. She was not to knock it over, or else he wouldn't just spank her, he would whip her. In order to do this so that the children wouldn't hear, he would make her go out naked into the garden and they would enter the garage. There, he would thrash her with a belt, usually giving her thirty very hard blows across the buttocks. It was no laughing matter. With a towel stuffed into

her mouth, Laura would moan and fling herself about, but she never attempted to escape her chastisement. Bent over the bonnet of the 2CV, she would receive her due. As soon as it was over, a very horny Bob would fuck her in both holes, and this would hurt her terribly because of her smarting buttocks. Once that was over, he would lead her back into the house, still naked, even if it was raining or snowing, with her grumbling under her breath.

"God, you're so cruel, Bob. You hit me really hard. I'll have bruises for a month!"

"Who cares, since you show your arse only to me, right?"

"Oh Bob, Bob, why are you so mean to me?"

"Because you love it," retorted the former barman. And he wasn't lying. She loved it! But not to the extent of deliberately knocking over the glass he had placed on her back before buggering her. She much preferred him to sodomise her here than on the bonnet of the car after flogging her.

And so she would open herself up and hold her breath. With a buttered finger, he would grease her anus and gallantly (he was always terribly polite when he buggered her) ask her if she was ready.

"Yes, Bob," whispered the pharmacist, "I'm wide open. You can stick it in."

He would pop it in in one go; she was so turned on and buttered that it would just slip in, even though he was hung like a horse.

~

Meanwhile, upstairs, the twins were bidding each other goodnight in a not altogether dissimilar manner. Bertrande,

with her buttocks raised and her nightie around her armpits, was receiving Bertrand's anal homage. They didn't have any butter so they merely used saliva. The brother would rim his sister for a long time and when he felt that she was sufficiently open and relaxed, he would stand up and put it in.

"Oh, aren't we disgusting!" giggled Bertrande when she felt his penis enter her arse. "When I think that Mum and Bob are in front of the telly; if they only knew!"

They would snigger stupidly, while listening to the distant sound of the television. They would take their time. Bertrande liked it to last a while with her brother; his slender penis never hurt her like the others, and with him she never felt any regret after her orgasm. They were too close, too alike. It helped that he would masturbate her while he buggered her, and he was very good at that. Much better than his cousins or his mates. The only thing on those guys' minds was to shoot their load. They just wanted to come in her mouth or in her bum, very quickly, while making lewd jokes. It was much more refined with her brother, and a lot more perverse.

As soon as they heard that the TV had been switched off, Bertrand would accelerate and fill up her bowels with come. Then they would exchange a tender sibling kiss and Bertrand would return to his bedroom next door, while Bébé went off to expel the semen in the toilet. A short while later, she would hear her mother and Bob talking quietly to avoid waking the children and she would stretch voluptuously in her cosy bed and think how lucky they were, her brother and her, to live in this delightful family nest. She would fall asleep, sucking her thumb like a baby. For Bébé loved to have something in her mouth. And when she wasn't sucking penises, she would settle for her thumb.

By dint of sucking, her teeth had become a little deformed. They would protrude slightly, like those of a rabbit, and her lower lip was also slightly misshapen and would hang as if she was constantly pouting. Bob would sometimes think, "That girl has a mouth that could suck doorknobs." But if she hadn't been Laura's daughter, it wouldn't have been doorknobs that he would have given her to suck.

Nor had it been a doorknob that she'd been sucking when he had caught her in the kitchen, kneeling in front of that idiot Jéréme...

CHAPTER FOUR: BÉBÉ AGREES TO BE A GOOD GIRL

B ut that night, there was no question of Bébé playing at 'pervy beddy-byes' with her brother. For one thing, there was that unexpected guest, 'Ernest the ex-con', and more importantly, there was that bastard Bob whom she would have to keep sweet. She noticed, as she approached the door, that he was imperiously questioning her with his eyes. So as to ensure that he knew that she would be back, she imploringly repeated, to her mother's surprise, "I'll just be a second, yeah, just a second... I'm just going for a pee."

"She's acting strangely tonight," said Mrs Desjardins as soon as her daughter had left the room. "I wonder why. It can't be her period already."

Bob shrugged. Ernest and Bertrand came back at this point, having fixed the washbasin, and so he didn't have to reply.

In her room, Bébé was looking at herself in the mirror. She was muttering to herself. "Are you going to do it? You have to," she said to the flushed girl facing her, "otherwise that bastard will spill the beans. God, I hate that nasty piece of work! I've never hated anyone so much. But I've gotta do it. I don't have a choice."

And with those words, she took off her knickers. Then, in front of the mirror, she opened her legs and parted her labia to check whether her vagina was clean. She noticed that she was all wet and this made her feel dirty. She was disgusted at the

thought that Bob had leered at her. She wiped herself angrily with a handkerchief then turned around and, with sordid coquettishness, she looked at her 'big fat bum', as Bertrand called it. The sight of her buxom behind always made her feel like laughing stupidly and pathologically in a way that left her all limp. She let her dress fall back and went to the bathroom to pee.

~

Once she had finished, she decided against putting her knickers back on and went back downstairs to join the others. She expected to hear the cheerful sound of voices, instead of which she heard only Mozart's Eine Kleine Nachtmusik. When she entered the lounge, she felt a pang of distress. There was only Bob in the room, sprawled on the sofa, still reading his paper, which he put down as soon as he saw her.

"Well, what about the others? Where is everyone?" asked Bébé.

"They're in the garage," replied Bob. "Your mother's showing Ernest the 2CV... You know it's got a dodgy distributor."

"Is Bertrand with them?"

She was terrified at the thought that her time had come.

"He's with them. We're alone," said Bob, "it's just the two of us..." he drawled, full of smutty innuendo. Bébé wasn't sure how to behave.

"You should change that CD," suggested Bob, as if to prompt her what to do next. "Mozart's not really my thing. Put something more upbeat on, like The Police or Madonna."

Without looking at him, Bébé went over to the CD rack and crouched with her knees together. She felt hot all over.

Bob waited, his paper lowered. Then, still looking away at the CDs, she turned her body towards him and opened her thighs. The blood rushed to her head. Her pussy opened up, warm and wet. She stayed absolutely still like this with her hand on the rack and her eyes lowered. She was as red as a beetroot. From the sofa, Bob was no longer smiling but was staring at what she displayed: a wide-open slit surrounded with hair. She knew what he was thinking: that she had removed her knickers just for him. Well, it was true, wasn't it? She felt deeply ashamed and hated herself for it. She felt as if she was selling herself. From beneath her eyelashes, she noticed that he shifted in his seat so as to get a better view of her crotch, and she spread her legs even wider and arched her back to offer him a good view.

As she was exhibiting herself so shamelessly, she felt tears of humiliation stinging her eyes. She sniffed loudly, like a little girl.

"Well then," said Bob in an oddly hoarse voice, "can't you find those CDs?"

She shook her head and the tears rolled down her cheeks. Her chest heaved with a sob.

"Don't cry," said Bob, "I won't tell your Mum anything; provided you're nice to me, you've nothing to worry about. Is that all right with you? Will you be a good girl?"

"Yes, Bob, I'll be a good girl."

"Then you've got nothing to worry about. It's settled."

He got up from the sofa and patted the seat in an inviting way.

"Come and sit down. I'll look for those CDs."

Bébé stood up and went to sit down. She was sobbing quietly. Bob crouched by the rack. He'd quickly replaced Mozart with

Prince. Sitting on the floor, he looked up at his step-daughter and noticed with delight that she had kept her legs wide open. Her slit was gaping a little in her bush. She was still snivelling, but she was showing him her pussy. He feasted his eyes for a while, then slowly got up and sat next to her. He savoured the moment with an expert eye.

"Sit over there, you'll be more comfortable to listen to the music," he said, gesturing towards the corner of the sofa, next to the armrest. She leaned back against it. He had lifted one of her ankles and she could feel him removing her shoes.

"There, you can put your feet up now. Make yourself comfortable. And stop crying. I won't tell your mother anything. We're friends, OK?"

"Yes, Bob," sobbed Bébé, "we're friends..." Oh, how she hated herself! She nestled against the armrest and let her step-father bend her knees so that her feet rested on the sofa. She was thus in virtually the same position as the one she adopted in bed, when she pretended to be asleep while waiting for her brother. Her eyes lowered, she watched as Bob hitched up her dress. She lifted her buttocks so that he could slide it under her.

"If I keep schtum," continued Bob, "we'll often be friends, like now, right?"

"Yes, Bob," hiccuped Bébé, "if you say nothing, we'll be friends, every time you feel like it."

Once her skirt had been pushed up, her step-father leaned over to look at her gaping slit. Bébé watched him with wide eyes and burning cheeks. She was feeling increasingly turned on despite herself.

"Since we're friends, you can tell me, you know; you haven't

done it just with Jéréme, have you? You've done it with the others as well, haven't you?"

"Yes, Bob, with the others as well."

"All of them?"

"Yes, Bob, all of them..."

"All they need to do is ask, right?"

She bowed her head. She was fiddling with the hem of her skirt and made sure that her thighs were spread as wide as possible. Horrified, she realised that she was dribbling.

"I knew it!" said Bob, caressing her pubic hair with his index finger. "I knew that if so many boys came here, it was to see you. They're attracted here like bees to a honeypot. And tell me, Bébé, is that the only thing you do with them?"

"No, Bob... we do other things as well..."

Bob's finger was caressing her furrow. She held her breath.

"But what about your virginity? You haven't..."

"Oh no, Bob, I wouldn't lose that!"

"May I check? I can't see very well."

"Of course you can, Bob, of course."

She hated the sound of her voice as she uttered those words; she sounded like a servile little cry-baby. As if he was opening a ripe fig, her bastard of a step-father parted her labia and gently inserted the tip of his index finger into her vagina. Bébé winced.

"Honest, Bob," she whined, "it's the truth, I never let them put it in there, never! Not even Bertrand! I promise."

When she saw the stunned look on her step-father's face, she understood that she had just dropped a huge clanger. He had never imagined that she could be up to anything with her own brother. How bloody stupid she'd been to give herself up so easily! She heard him catch his breath.

"For God's sake... even with her brother!" he whispered. And he pushed his finger further in.

"Please, Bob, not here, not in front... please!"

"Not in front?" He was certainly getting his fair share of surprises. "Is it OK from behind?"

Bébé's eloquent silence and her embarrassed flushed expression made him smile wanly.

"Well, well. You're a dark horse!"

Bob stopped checking her narrow vagina and gently touched her clitoris. She flinched and held her breath. Her ears were burning. Bob started to laugh softly and played a little with her clit.

"Looks like you like that, eh? Answer me!"

"Yes, Bob, I prefer that."

"Look at me," he said, "don't look down. You're not as shy with them when they masturbate you, are you?"

She reluctantly obeyed and looked straight into her step-father's eyes. He was as red-faced as she was and he made her think of a pervy little boy. While he fiddled with her clit, he explored her cunt and her arse. Enraged against her own body, she felt she was going to come; panicking, she begged him hoarsely, "Bob, Bob, please, stop, please, not now, Mum..."

He stopped wanking her and sniggered. His finger touched her wrinkled anus.

"So they take you up here, do they? Answer me. Don't lie. I can check."

Shamefully, Bébé nodded.

"Yes, Bob, up there. Only from behind. They say it doesn't count."

She saw her step-father smile smugly.

"You little slut," he said, "I bet you even do it with your

brother when he goes up to say goodnight... and your stupid mother who finds that cute..."

"Oh, don't tell her anything, Bob! If we're friends, you won't tell her, will you? Please don't tell Mum. I'll do anything..."

He bossily put a hand over her mouth. The sound of voices in the corridor announced the return of the others. A frowning Bob gestured for her to stand up. She quickly obeyed and noticed a damp stain on the sofa. Quick as a flash, Bob covered it with a cushion. Bébé pulled down her skirt, put on her shoes and sat on a cushion on the floor, with her back to Bob who had picked up his paper.

"You should have seen how he fixed that car!" gushed Laura. "In a flash! Your cousin really has nimble fingers."

"You should tell him to have a look at the fridge while he's at it. It shouldn't frost up so quickly," joked Bob.

From the sound of his voice, it was obvious that he was in excellent humour.

Chapter Five: The spanking

It was already quite late in the evening and after coffee and liqueurs, Bob, his cousin, Bertrand and Laura were still in the lounge. Bébé had gone to bed a good hour ago, but her brother seemed in no hurry to follow her. The truth was that the ex-con, who was in high spirits following a few glasses of sloe gin, was teaching him card tricks. It was a joy to see him handle the cards; they fluttered between his hands and did whatever he wanted them to do. That Ernest was most definitely king of the three card trick; he no longer resembled a priest when he was shuffling cards, and Bertrand thought he was much more fun this way.

While admiring Ernest's skilfulness, Bob was thinking about his step-daughter. He had rarely felt as horny as this evening when the little slut had spread her legs to show him her pussy. He remembered the pleasure he had felt on touching her slit while watching her cry. Girls who snivelled when you touched their thingummy were always the best lays. God, Bob was crazy about that little tart, he could think of only one thing, and that was to find a way of joining her upstairs, just for a moment. Just long enough to stick his big cock up her arse! He was certain that crafty little minx was a great fuck. His mouth was watering at the very thought. If she wanted to be 'friends' as she said, they would become 'friends' all right!

Bob could stand it no longer and stood up. His wife, who was having a great time as Ernest was teaching her the rudiments of the three card trick, looked at him in puzzlement.

"Carry on with what you're doing," grunted Bob, "I'll be back in a minute. I'm just going for a quick fag in the garden."

He would sometimes go into the garden for a cigarette, so Laura didn't think twice about it. Bob was like everyone else, he had his whims. Just as he was leaving the room, he thought of a surefire way of preventing Bertrand from going to his sister's room.

"Wait for me, all of you, I'm just going for a quick smoke, and then, why don't we play poker, the four of us?"

"Oh no," protested Laura, "that's a mobster's game!"

"Oh come on, Laura, we won't play for real money, just for laughs. For matchsticks."

"Oh go on, Mum," insisted Bertrand, "it'll be fun. A game of poker!"

The silly boy was already imagining himself telling all his mates that he'd played poker with an ex-convict. Bob chuckled to himself and left the lounge. He walked down the corridor, pushed the front door and closed it again without leaving the house. He quickly removed his shoes and carried them as he went upstairs. His heart was beating so hard it was almost painful. Why was he getting himself into such a state? He didn't want to show that little brat the effect she was having on him. As if the little slut didn't already know! Why else would she have shown him her pussy? And what about last summer? Bloody hell, just the thought of last summer made his blood boil!

"I'll make her pay for last summer, and a heavy price too!"

While he tiptoed upstairs like a burglar, keeping his ears open for the slightest sound, Bob remembered the way that little minx had teased him during the August heatwave the previous year.

On the pretext that the heat was unbearable that summer in her south-facing bedroom, Bébé had got into the habit of doing her homework topless. She would deliberately leave her door open to create a draught. The first time her step-father had walked past her door and had seen her like this, writing at her desk with her pretty boobs jutting out insolently in front of her, he had been rooted to the spot, such was his surprise. Those breasts of hers were simply magnificent, they had made his mouth water. Bertrande had slyly looked up at him and, pouting like a capricious child and fluttering her eyelashes, had simpered, "Hey, Bob, you don't mind if I stay like this to swot for my end-of-year exam, do you? It's boiling! I can't stand clothes against my skin, the sweat just pours off me and I get all sticky!"

But judging from her crafty and flushed expression, he gathered that it wasn't just because of the heat that she was exhibiting herself in this way. As soon as she had noticed her step-father staring greedily at her breasts, Bébé had arched her back coquettishly to draw attention to her youthful charms. The hardened nipples of her already heavy (she took after her mother in that respect) and gorgeous boobs were pointing straight at Bob like two pink bullets. However, he realised that while she was impudently offering herself up to his curiosity, she was also keeping a watchful eye on him. He would have liked to carry on regardless, after having let drop some contemptuous remark, but he had been frozen to the spot by this lovely sight. Feeling incapable of detaching himself from this vision, he had cleared his throat.

"Of course, it's hot..." he had conceded. "I'd like to wander around starkers as well, same as you. But it wouldn't be such a pretty sight, that's for sure!"

She had giggled as girls do at that age, causing her lovely boobs to swing and he had the impression that the nipples were pointing even more.

"Oh Bob," she had whispered, sucking on her pen, "you mustn't say things like that. I'm almost your daughter after all!"

"No, I haven't forgotten. And what about your mother, by the way? What would she say?" Bébé's eyes had widened innocently.

"When she's home, I'll definitely put on a tee-shirt. I know she's a bit old-fashioned. But you, are you sure it doesn't bother you? You must tell me, I can always close the door. Or else I can put on a bra... Because it gets so hot when there isn't a draught."

That little tart was taking the mickey! He knew full well that if he ever made an improper move on her, she would cry rape and go running to Mummy. Bob managed to control himself. After all, he was getting an eyeful, it was better than nothing.

"Oh, I don't mind. But keep an eye out for your mother. And what about your brother?"

"Bertrand? You must be joking, Bob! He's already seen them, believe me! Come on now, you're forgetting that we're twins. We have nothing to hide from each other. I can be naked in front of him, and vice versa. We're identical... well, almost... but he's my brother, it doesn't count. It's different with you, you're Mum's husband, and it bothers me, I assure you, to show them to you. But it's so damn hot!"

With a throaty laugh, she had put her pen back in her

mouth and had licked the cap with the tip of her little pink tongue. Bob would have given his right arm to give her a good spanking. He would have thoroughly enjoyed reddening her big bum. And those lovely firm, plump tits... He felt like biting into them. With his 'big-brotherly' smile, Bob had gritted his teeth and had gone back downstairs.

During that month of August, taking advantage of the heatwave, Bébé had constantly flaunted her breasts in front of him. As soon as they were alone in the house, she would innocently wander around topless. She would come down to the kitchen for a glass of water wearing just a tiny pair of knickers that barely hid her pussy and that had wedged themselves between her buttocks. When she saw Bob, she would pretend to be surprised and cover her breasts with her outstretched fingers. But try as she might, her fingers were far too small to hide her generous charms. In fact, because she splayed her fingers, her big pink nipples would be insolently framed between them; thus, instead of hiding them, she seemed to be offering them to him like two plump ripe fruit.

"Oh, you're there, Bob," she'd say, her big eyes making her look like a frightened doe (this was a trick of hers that she'd practised many times in front of the mirror). I didn't know. Sorry, I don't have much on. Don't mind me, I'm just getting some cold water from the fridge."

With a falsely apologetic sigh, she made no effort to cover up her blossoming young femininity and would bend over to search inside the fridge, with her tits swinging between her arms. The rear view wasn't bad either; between her ample buttocks, whose creaminess was highlighted by her tanned back and thighs, he could see the back of her knickers, which were all creased and damp with sweat and penetrating her

buttocks like a piece of cord. Feeling her step-father's gaze on her behind, Bébé would bend over even lower, and while pretending to consider what she would have, would shamelessly spread her legs. What an arse she had, that dirty little brat! Bob felt crazed, he would break out into a cold sweat. Sometimes the little slut would bend over so low that, on either side of the thin pink nylon string, he could glimpse the edges of the dark circle of her anus surrounded with tiny hairs. He had to get a grip on himself so as not to leap on her and his self-control took so much effort that he would dig his nails into his palms, to the point where they would bleed. As soon as she had gone back upstairs, humming to herself, swinging her buttocks and her tits up the stairs, Bob, who had followed her with his eyes, open-mouthed like a half-wit, would swear under his breath and run over to the sink for a wank to release the tension.

He had flogged the bishop so much that month because of that little pest that, come the evenings, he would be useless to Laura, and she had even commented acrimoniously on it. He had had to blame it on the heat.

In a way, Bob had felt almost grateful when it got cooler. He no longer saw Bébé wander around in her birthday suit right under his nose and he was able to think of something else. Later on, and this aroused his suspicions, his step-daughter became a lot more shy around him. He was almost certain then that she had tried to set him a trap by exhibiting herself like that so that, if need be, she could complain to her mother at the slightest hint of molestation. The twins didn't like him and it was an open secret that they had always resented their mother remarrying a much younger man.

He knew then that he had been right not to trust her.

But that evening, things had changed. He had that little darling cornered. He would show her what a real man was like. Of course, he would have to be careful; Laura wasn't stupid. He was living the high life here and he didn't want to jeopardise that. But he trusted himself and he knew that he was up to the job. He reached the first floor landing and felt daft carrying his shoes. He put them back on and opened the door to Bébé's room. He didn't even bother to knock, he wanted to show her who was boss from now on and that she was at his disposal.

He had expected to find her in bed and was surprised to see her sitting at her desk. "Aren't you in bed yet?" That's all he could think of saying. He saw her blush violently and shake her head.

"I was revising my maths. I didn't get a chance, this afternoon..." She looked at him, wide-eyed, as he closed the door quietly behind him. He had never come into her room before. They sized each other up. Tensely hostile, she held his gaze. He had the impression that she was eluding him again.

"What do you want, Bob? Why are you here?"

"I have to talk to you. Have you forgotten what happened in the kitchen?"

She lowered her head and shrugged sullenly.

"What about Mum? Where is she?" she asked cautiously.

"Downstairs. Ernest's teaching them card tricks."

Bébé looked thoughtful. Bob didn't have time to think up a riposte. He didn't trust the little minx; she looked stupid but she knew how to manage her interests.

"I've had time to ponder over what happened in the kitchen. And especially what you told me, about your brother. How he buggered you and all that."

He smugly noticed Bébé going bright red and continued, "I think it's best if I tell your mother everything. It's not a good idea, at your age, to do that sort of thing with your brother. You two have to be separated, it's not a wholesome situation."

As he spoke, he noticed Bébé's face gradually changing expression. If she had thought that she could pull out of the game, she now realised she had to give in to him, and fast!

"You see, I told myself that it was in your interest. You don't seem to realise that those bastards are taking advantage of you."

"Bob, I assure you that I'm always consenting. They've never forced me," protested Bébé in a panic-stricken voice.

"That's even worse," said Bob. "To be perfectly honest, that kind of thing can mess you up. A brother who buggers his sister, no, frankly, it shocks me, even though I'm usually pretty open-minded when it comes to sex. I've got to protect you against yourself."

Bébé frantically got up from her desk, ran over to her step-father and grabbed his arms.

"No, Bob, I beg you, please," she beseeched him, "don't tell Mum! Bob, please! You said we'd be friends."

"Friends? Have you seen how you welcome me when I come into your room to say goodnight? Sure, you'd rather it was your brother!"

His sobbing step-daughter returned to the attack and clung to him in an attempt to make him relent; when she saw that this left him cold, she dropped onto her knees and hugged his legs.

"Bob, Bob," she sobbed, "don't tell Mum. It was wrong of me, I'm very sorry and I won't do it again. You can come into

my room any time you want. I promise. I won't sulk any more. I swear, Bob. I swear on the Virgin Mary."

Her face was level with his groin and she threw her neck backwards to implore him; tears were running down her cheeks. A phenomenal erection lifted Bob's penis. God, how he wanted her! He bent down and brutally hoisted her up by the breasts, so roughly that she moaned, and holding her thus by the tits, he set her back on her feet.

"Stop moaning, all right? And leave the Virgin Mary out of this."

Bob hated mixing religion and sex. He had a sense of decency regarding such matters.

"OK, Bob," hiccuped Bébé, "I agree to everything you ask, provided you don't tell Mum. Ow, you're hurting me, you're gripping them too hard, I'm going to be covered in bruises."

He relaxed his grip a little and smiled wanly. She passively let him knead her breasts.

"Do you remember last summer, when you deliberately teased me by showing off your tits?"

She looked down and chewed her lip.

"It was wrong of me, Bob, I admit it, I was doing it on purpose to bug you."

"And why did you want to bug me, eh, why? Flaunting your tits and arse as soon as we were alone?"

"I don't know, Bob. Sometimes I have urges like that. I have the urge to be..."

"Yes?"

"... naughty, if you like... do you know what I mean?"

"Like with Jéréme in the kitchen?"

Bébé didn't answer.

"Do you know what you deserve?" he asked hoarsely. She

shook her head and didn't dare look at him.

"Do you know what naughty girls deserve?" he continued in an increasingly husky voice. She looked up at him, seemingly mesmerised by the expression on her step-father's face. She slowly shook her head.

"A spanking," murmured Bob, "that's what naughty girls deserve, a spanking on their naked bottom."

"Here?" whispered Bébé. "Oh, Bob, here? Now? Come on, you're crazy!"

"Would you rather I went downstairs and told your mother?"

"No, Bob, no. But I really don't think it's a good idea, Bob, I assure you. What if Mum…"

"Take off your knickers, hurry up. They're waiting for me downstairs. We're supposed to be playing poker."

Bébé chewed on her thumb.

"I… er…. didn't put them back on, Bob. Since earlier, I mean, I'm not wearing any."

"Oh yes, I'd forgotten," he sniggered. He turned her around and pointed to the bed.

"Get on there and show me your bottom."

"Oh God, Bob, what are you asking me? I'm ashamed."

"Do as you're told."

Bébé knelt on the bed, leant forwards and pulled up her dress. When she had bared her arse, she felt a hot wave wash over her and uttered a muffled cry.

"Spread your legs," grunted Bob, "open your buttocks, arch your back. Everything's got to be nice and open. It's got to breathe!"

With an iron grip, he forced her to prostrate herself by pressing her face into the pillow. He felt jubilant at the sight of her submission, with her arse drawn up high, her legs wide apart and all her pubic

hair on show. What he didn't know was that this was the exact same position that Bertrand would make her adopt so as to bugger her. She started to choke with arousal. Her intrigued step-father was fondling her anus and vagina. She was fired up; he didn't have to 'open her up', she 'opened up' of her own accord. Her anus and her vulva were very dilated, as if they were being pushed out from the inside.

"You're going to get your spanking. Don't think I'll change my mind. Stay like that, whatever you do, don't move."

"I won't move, Bob. Oh God, I'm sure you can see everything!"

She certainly wasn't hiding anything. Between her pubic hair, the pink flesh of her vulva, which was all wet from her secretions, was gaping lusciously and he could even see some red flesh peeping out from her anus, revealing the secret flesh of her bowel. He sat down on the edge of the bed and feeling overcome by emotion, he rolled up his sleeves. Voluptuously, he began to tap her buttocks. He gave her short, sharp slaps that made her flesh jiggle. At each slap he dealt her burgeoning behind, he delighted in seeing the reactions of her gaping wet cunt, as rapid spasms shuddered through it. As soon as his hand made contact, his step-daughter's anus and vagina would tighten fearfully, but would then re-open with even greater eagerness.

He was amused and aroused at this sight and his slaps became more forceful. He started to smack her thighs, inching higher and higher.

"Oh God," sobbed Bébé (she was sobbing from excitement and arousal, not from pain, even though Bob was spanking her hard now, she loved it, it drove her completely wild). "Oh God, Bob, be careful, don't make too much noise... Mum will hear..."

"You like it, don't you?" sniggered Bob, hitting her hard between the legs, which made her utter an astonished groan, which she quelled by biting her pillow.

"I knew you'd enjoy being spanked, you disgusting little slut! That'll teach you to suck off boys. Filthy little creature!"

He hit her again squarely on her crack and felt the moist and smarting flesh give way under his palm. At each slap, Bébé would give out a muffled moan and would savagely bite the pillowcase. She felt overcome by a dark exhilaration which she communicated to Bob who responded by hitting her harder and harder.

"Dirty little bitch who showed me her crack earlier, while her mother was practically next door!"

"Oh Bob, that was so that you wouldn't tell her! Don't hit me so hard, please, you're making too much noise, they'll hear us. My behind is on fire, it's burning all over, I've never felt this before! It's as if I'm having some kind of fit."

Bébé felt incredibly aroused and remembered that those very sounds that were filling her ears every time Bob's hand whacked one of her buttock cheeks or her crotch were the very same sounds that sometimes emanated from her mother's room. At the time, she had wondered what they could possibly be. Now she knew: Bob had been spanking her mother! She found this idea deeply disturbing. She had never before felt so aroused, even when playing with her brother or her cousins. Her arse felt literally on fire and, between her legs, it was even worse.

"Bob, Bob," she whimpered, "I beg you, stop, it's driving me crazy, and I'm scared Mum's going to hear."

He finally seemed to realise the risk they would take if he got even more carried away; he wouldn't be able to control

himself and he would probably go too far. He thought of the others who were waiting for him downstairs. He hoped Ernest was amusing them with his card tricks.

"Stay like that. Show me your arse."

"Yes, Bob, yes, I'm showing it to you. You see? I'm being a good girl. See how I'm showing it off to you."

Bébé arched her back in an outrageous manner, straining to make the internal flesh of her vagina bulge to such an extent that her labia curled away a little. It looked like a big glistening gash between the hairs.

"Can you see it, Bob? Can you?"

"I can see it all right. You should be ashamed. Everything's open and wet. So wet! You should be ashamed of yourself, you naughty girl."

He ran his finger through her slit and pressed on her clitoris.

"Aaaaaahhhhh..." went Bébé, "rrrhhhaaaaahhh! Ohhhhhh..." she sighed, "Bob! Bob! Oh God in Heaven!"

He looked at the wetness that was pouring out of her slit, which was puffy from the spanking. His step-daughter was wriggling her crimson arse, her anus silently beckoning him by dilating like a flower's corolla.

"And my arsehole," she whispered, "can you see it as well? Eh? Can you see it? Oh, if you only knew how it prickles, it feels as if it's on fire! Oh, you hit me so hard... You're so mean to me, you horrible man!"

"Mean to you? Don't be silly. That was just a taster. You wait till we're alone in the house. Just the two of us. Then I'll properly deal with your big arse!"

"Oh yes, Bob," approved Bébé, in a delighted voice, "oh yes, you can deal with it. I'll let you spank me as often as you like.

But we'll have to look out for Bertrand, yeah? He mustn't go telling Mum. Promise me, Bob? He mustn't find out, OK?"

"We'll see," grunted Bob, "I'll let you know. And now, get off that bed, you dirty slut. On your knees. I'm going to give you your dessert."

CHAPTER SIX: THE BLOW-JOB

Bébé stood up; meekly and adoringly, she looked up at her step-father. She was as red as a beetroot and her mouth was all swollen.

"Oh, you hit my bottom so hard, Bob," she simpered, gingerly feeling her behind, "you hurt me a lot. My bottom's all burning!" She lowered her eyes. "And you saw all my holes... you touched me all over, Bob, absolutely everywhere, naughty Bob!"

She let out an embarrassed titter.

"You took advantage of me, didn't you, you didn't just give me a spanking. I felt you putting your finger inside me. And not just behind, but in front as well! I felt it, you know."

"What? How dare you! You insolent little minx! I'll teach you. Get down on your knees, d'you hear? Now! And apologise!"

As if she had been expecting this command, Bébé immediately sank down on her knees in front of her step-father.

"I'm sorry, Bob, I'm sorry. I wasn't complaining, honest. I won't do it again, I swear I won't."

"And what is it you won't do again? Can you tell me? Bring your arm down. Put your hands behind your back."

Bébé obeyed. Once she'd put her hands behind her back, she arched herself to stick her breasts out, but she kept her eyes lowered. She remained silent, as if she was considering how to behave towards her step-father.

"I won't suck off my cousins in the kitchen, Bob," she whispered at last. "I promise. Not in the kitchen, nor in

my bedroom, nor in the garden. Not even in the shower, Bob. Nowhere."

"And what else?"

Giggling nervously, Bébé put her thumb in her mouth and nibbled it. Suddenly, she stared straight ahead like a doll. Right under her nose, Bob had started to unbutton his fly. He wasn't in a hurry. Trembling with impatience, Bébé looked at him.

"And..." she murmured, "I won't let my brother or any other boy put their thing in my bum. I promise, Bob, never again! Even if they insist, I'll just say no. Even if, as they often do when I don't want to, they all hold me down and there's one who's holding my hands, another who's pulling down my knickers, while a third one parts my buttocks to force it in, well, even then, I won't let them! I won't let them rape me any more, Bob, I swear. And I won't even let them do it to me if I really want it. I promise!"

She fell silent and took her thumb out of her mouth; her step-father had just put two fingers inside his trousers.

"And what else?" he asked.

"I won't say a word if you touch my holes when you spank me," whispered a goggling Bébé. "And I won't get the hump when you come into my room. You can come as often as you like and do anything you like to me."

"Really anything?"

"Yes, Bob, absolutely anything. I mean it! You only have to ask. Not even that, just tell me what you'd like. How you want me, if I should take off my knickers so that you can punish me better, and all that. I'll do whatever you like." She stopped suddenly and boundless amazement showed on her face. A moan of pleasure quavered between her lips.

"Oh, God, Bob! Oh God, but... Oh, Bob! Bob! It's massive! Oh yes, show me the whole thing, pull it all out. Oh God, I mean it, I've never seen anything like it!"

Indeed, the tool that her step-father had just pulled out from his trousers was so impressively large that Bébé couldn't believe her eyes. She felt a pang of envy and understood why her mother was so crazy about her second husband, and why he had her wrapped around his little finger.

"Look at that boner!" gloated Bob. "Just look!"

Between two fingers, he squeezed the tip of his penis and peeled back the foreskin to reveal the glans.

"Oh yes, Bob, yes, show me your thing, I like it when boys do that, it's all red... It's gross but I like it. Blimey, yours is so big! The head, I mean, it's so red!"

"You like my tool? It's a Colt 36, that's what it is! A Python 357! A large calibre weapon; yep, it must be a bit different to the 6.35s you're used to playing with. Look at that, eh?" The head was glowing in the light of the bedside lamp like a living ember.

"Oh Bob, can I? Please? Can I touch it a little, Bob? Please! Just for a moment."

She tremblingly raised her hand and waited for her step-father's permission. He moved towards her and she greedily grabbed the big rod of flesh. She uttered a cry of delight.

"Oh, it's so hard as well! Can I, Bob? Can I?"

"Of course you can play with it, I'm lending it to you."

"Oh, I love it so much, Bob... so much that it makes me warm all over when boys let me touch it. I'm so glad we're friends now, you and I. We'll have lots of fun, behind Mum's back."

With both hands, she rapturously fondled his balls and his big,

bare-headed cock. She couldn't get enough of it. Inquisitively, she squeezed the elastic and clammy flesh of the bared glans.

"That's the bit I like best, Bob, that big red bit there... Boys jump when I touch it. You like it as well, don't you, you like your thing being touched... I can guess from your movements, you know. Hey, Bob, can I... with the tip of my tongue... just once?"

"Course you can," said Bob, who was beginning to lose it a bit. "You can lick it as much as you like... that big lollipop's yours, all yours."

Bloody hell, she was driving him insane, absolutely insane! She was really cock-mad, he'd never seen such gluttony in his life. He stared at her as she stuck out her little pink tongue, as delicate as a cat's, and slowly licked the underside of the head. An exquisite sensation tickled his flesh and ran up his spine before exploding in his neck. He felt his toes splaying in his shoes and gasped.

"Oh Bob, I can't control myself any more, I've got to put the whole thing in my mouth, do you mind? I want it too much. Don't worry, I won't bite it, I'm used to it."

Without further ado, she voraciously opened her mouth. When he saw the glint of her pearly-white teeth, Bob recoiled and shivered in icy fear. That silly goose seemed so loopy that he suddenly feared that she might bite off his cock, and his instinct was to push her away. But she beat him to it and gulped it down to the root.

Bob gasped. It was incredible! He must be dreaming. That mouth was like velvet, and so meltingly tender! And so warm! Her little tongue circled his penis perfectly. He shivered all over in bursts, as if he was having a malaria attack. This cannibal was sucking out his soul, she was emptying him

of his essence. He sobbed in ecstasy and devoutly stroked her head.

It wasn't for show; one could tell that she really enjoyed it. She was gorging herself, pigging out. With both hands, she clutched his balls and plunged the whole thing right to the back of her throat so that he could feel her uvula against his glans and he wondered how she managed not to choke. Then she would lean back and squeeze it between her lips, sliding dizzyingly high, and it was truly divine. When it was almost out and there were only her lips forming a warm elastic ring around the glans which was swollen to bursting point, she'd explore the hole at the end of his cock with the tip of her tongue and he felt as if his heart was flipping over. It was all too much.

"Gently does it, Bébé, gently does it," he begged her, "take your time, my love... there's no rush, we don't have a train to catch."

Christ, he now understood why all the lads in the neighbourhood came running to the house like a pack of rutting hounds. She obviously drove those brats wild. They probably dreamt of her velvet mouth day and night. If she carried on like this, he'd certainly risk a heart attack. Suddenly, while she was putting the finishing touches around the glans, Bob remembered what she had said about boys taking off her knickers and buggering her by force. He realised that he too could have it off with this little peach. He'd just have to go easy on her, given the dimensions of his tool, but she wouldn't say no. He had reason to believe that her arse was as greedy as her mouth. He remembered her swollen anus which had turned itself inside out like a flower when he had slapped it.

"Good God," he thought, "even if it means that I have to

die on the spot from heart failure, even if it's the last thing I do on this fucking earth, I have to bugger that little sow. I have to fuck her in the arse! Then my life won't have been wasted. Ahrrrggghhh!" She was nibbling him! The crafty little minx was nibbling him and it was unbearably exquisite. He no longer experienced any anxiety. She knew how to use her pearly-whites, she was an expert, she wouldn't lose her head. Her tiny teeth were pecking at him with amazing speed, it was quite simply a miraculous sensation. He had never experienced anything remotely as good, even with the most reputable whores, the queens of blow-jobs, those that charged three times as much to give head as for a regular trick.

"Oh yes, yes, with your teeth... with your little gnashers," he moaned stupidly, while gyrating like a salsa dancer.

He'd bugger her later, this was just too delicious. And suddenly, it welled up, from behind, from beneath, it came from afar, from the depths of his loins, it swelled like a wave of fire, it lifted him onto his toes like a ballerina. He desperately thrashed around.

"Oh no, no," he implored, "oh fuck, it's coming, I can feel it's coming. I'm going to come!"

Bébé immediately took it out of her mouth.

"Oh no, Bob," she begged him, "please hold back, don't come just yet, I want to keep it in my mouth for a bit longer."

"Too late," panted her step-father, whose eyes were popping, "it's coming, hurry up for God's sake, I'm nearly there, it's going to come out, quickly, put it back in your mouth! Quickly!"

"But I want to suck it a bit longer."

"You can suck it to your heart's content later, but for now, I've got to come, it's urgent!"

Bébé distrustfully observed the fat glans that was bobbing

about from the spasms which were shaking his penis.

"You say that, but when's it's gone all soft, you won't want me to suck it any more. You men, you're all the same!"

"I'm not like them, I'll let you have it back, honest."

"Great!" exclaimed Bébé, clapping her hands. She delightedly burst out laughing.

"Do you swear? You'll let me have it? Oh I love it, I tell you, when it's soft and it goes hard in my mouth, that's what I like best... Oh, it's so nice with you, it's much better than with the others. Go on, put it in, and shoot it all in my mouth."

Clutching him with both hands, she shoved it in right to the back of her throat and sucked. Just in the nick of time. A phenomenal ejaculation wrenched his essence out of him. A white streak flashed across his brain. A second spurt of semen, as generous as the first, immediately gushed out of him. He was sure he was going to die. From the depths of his ecstasy, he was aghast to see that his step-daughter was swallowing, as it came, what he was expelling into her mouth. She was sucking him like an infant, swallowing every last drop. Finally, only when a last jolt made him gasp for breath and his balls were really empty, did she agree to let him go.

Holding his penis like a big over-ripe banana that was beginning to go limp, she rubbed the foreskin over the glans which was shiny with spit.

"Did you see? I swallowed it all. Look, I'm not having you on."

She opened her mouth wide to show him and stuck out her tongue like at the doctor's. He spotted a drop of semen on her uvula.

"There was so much of it! I enjoyed that, you know. I love

it when it gushes with such force. See? It's all soft now, naughty willy!"

Tittering childishly, Bébé shook the big flaccid penis from side to side. A last droplet of semen collected at the opening.

"Oh, there's a drop left, give it here, it's mine!"

Incredulously, he watched her catch the drop with the tip of her tongue. She really liked it. It was rare, even among the blow-job queens, to find a girl who appreciated the taste of semen. They would usually spit into a hankie and give themselves airs, saying it was sticky and tacky and disgusting; but not her, she was smacking her lips.

"And I like to lick here as well, you know... Underneath, where it smells strong."

Holding his dick in one hand, she lifted his balls with the other and started to forage around the hairy folds of skins, lapping up his sweat. She giggled hysterically.

"I'll even lick your arsehole if you like. Some boys like that. Oh, give it to me again, even if it's soft, I want it again. Shove it in deep. I want to swallow it all, even those big things there..."

She gorged herself on his flesh and began to chew away at his cock with muffled grunts.

Chapter Seven: A three-way quarrel

Kneeling before her step-father whose balls she was grasping with both hands, Bébé was sucking him off greedily. She could feel the flaccid cock that she was feasting on twitch back into life under her tongue. Bob was just standing there. They were both engrossed in their pleasure and had closed their eyes to concentrate better. They consequently did not see the door open; furthermore, they were so absorbed in their sensations that they didn't hear Laura approach them.

"Are you there, Bob? You're not in the garden. Your cousin's such a hoot. He's so funny. But... but... what are you up to? What are you doing on your knees, Bébé?"

The pharmacist froze in horror. Her own daughter... her husband...

"But... but... what's going on? Bob! Bébé! Stop it immediately!"

Dopey from his pleasure, Bob lazily half-opened his eyes and turned towards his wife, as slowly as if the scene had been filmed in slow-motion. It was like one of those science-fiction novels that he liked to read, where people aren't in the same 'temporal stasis'. He and Laura were no longer on the same plane.

"Good God," he thought sluggishly, "it's Laura! What the hell is she doing here? And why is she so cross? We're doing nothing wrong, I'm just having my trouser-snake polished."

He felt like laughing, stupidly, from the depths of his strange stupor. With the same cataleptic slowness, Bébé, who had

also noticed her mother's shrieks through the warm fog that enveloped her, let her step-father's huge penis slip out of her mouth with a feeling of waste. Why was this pain-in-the-neck bothering them during her favourite bit, when it was stiffening again in her mouth? She vindictively glared at her mother.

A stunned Laura was looking at Bébé's naked buttocks; she was surprised by how red they looked. It was winter, she couldn't have got sunburnt. Then she saw her husband's balls glistening with saliva. She uttered another outraged scream which made them both start. They were wide awake now. Bébé stood up quickly and fearfully backed away towards the bed.

Laura furiously punched her husband on the chest; he staggered backwards, stunned by her violence.

"Bastard! You bastard! Oh, so you were popping out to the garden for a fag, were you? Is that your idea of a smoke? With my own daughter! Under my roof! She's underage! But I'm not going to let it rest, I'll put you behind bars for this!"

"But Mum," said Bébé, "I'm not really underage, I'm sixteen!"

"You little slut! Are you taking his side?"

She slapped her daughter so hard that she spun around. Bébé fell onto the bed and winced as she landed on her behind that was still sore from the recent spanking. Rubbing herself, she cried out, "Don't hit me, Mum! Don't hit me! You've never hit me before!" And she started to sob like a little girl.

"That's clearly where I went wrong!" thundered her mother. "You're nothing but a shameless little tart!"

"But he made me do it, Mum! I swear he did. You see, I'm not lying, he gave me a spanking." She turned around to display her inflamed buttocks. "See, it's true. Look at the

state of me! My bum's all swollen, you've no idea how much it hurts."

"The little bitch," thought Bob, "how quickly she changes sides. She can see which way the wind is blowing all right!"

Her eyes goggling in horror, the pharmacist stared at the crimson bottom. She turned to her husband.

"You did this to her? You hit my daughter to force her to do... to do those filthy things?"

"What?" he said indignantly (he'd really had enough of this). "Don't listen to her. It's true that I gave her a spanking, but she deserved it. Do you know what I witnessed when I arrived with Ernest? Luckily, he didn't see anything. It would have given him funny ideas about my family! She was sucking off Jéréme in the kitchen. It's the truth! That's why I punished her, to teach her how to behave. And if it was only Jéréme, but he's just the tip of the iceberg!"

He stopped himself just in time, for he was about to mention Bertrand and Bébé's confession regarding their incestuous relationship. Why did he keep quiet? He couldn't explain why. He had very nearly let the cat out of the bag, but he had stopped in time. Why? Was it male solidarity? After all, her brother was right to take advantage of this slut. He would have done the same if he'd had a sister who was crazy about sodomy. In such circumstances, you don't stop to think about notions of right and wrong. You just have to fuck!

His mind was racing now. Things had never seemed so clear. His fate was at stake. By keeping silent about Bertrand, he was aware that he was keeping an ace up his sleeve, just in case it really all went pear-shaped.

"You did that? With your own cousin?" hissed Laura.

From the way her daughter shrugged sullenly, Laura knew

that her husband hadn't lied. Feeling that she was weakening, Bob drove the point home.

"And in the lounge earlier," he continued, "d'you remember when she supposedly went upstairs for a pee?"

Bébé threw him a hateful look. Laura Desjardins nodded slowly. She remembered perfectly well, especially because it had struck her as odd.

"So?"

"She went upstairs to take off her knickers, not to pee. After that, she kept showing me her bits, even when you were in the room. You should have seen her spreading her legs! Then when you went off with Ernest to fix the 2CV's distributor, she pulled her dress up to her neck to show it off better!"

"He's lying, Mum, it's him who pulled it up!"

"And the knickers?" asked her mother.

Bébé bowed her head.

"It's true that I'd taken off my knickers. It was so that he wouldn't tell you that he'd seen me with Jéréme. I thought that if I showed him my thingummy, he'd keep schtum. But that wasn't enough for him, he also wanted to touch it!"

Stunned, Laura Desjardins looked at each one in turn. Her head switched from one to the other as if she was watching a game of ping-pong.

"The reason I didn't tell you," pleaded her husband, "was because of Ernest; I didn't want to spoil the party. That's why I went upstairs to tell her that there was no point in her showing me her arse, because I'd still tell you the truth. That I wouldn't stoop to anything like that."

"What a coward!" thought Bébé. "Look how he's chickening out, how he's grovelling!" She was disgusted.

"And last summer," remembered Bob, "when it was so hot.

D'you know what she used to do? As soon as you were out, the second you were out of the door, she'd strip off and she'd wander around in front of me with her tits and arse on show. I could have killed the little slut! She showed me everything on purpose. Put yourself in my shoes, I'm only human after all. Well, even though she offered me her charms, I didn't give in to temptation. D'you know why? Precisely because she was underage. I thought to myself, she's not responsible for her actions, she's bonkers."

"Oh!" exclaimed Bébé indignantly.

"Is it not true that you ran around starkers?"

"At first I only took off my bra."

Her mother felt overwhelmed by this indirect confession and dropped onto the bed. Bob continued, gloatingly.

"You should have seen the knickers she wore, some transparent wisp of a thing that would get wedged between her buttocks; it was worse than if she'd been naked!"

"Shut up," said Laura softly, "please shut up. I've heard enough."

From Bébé's shamefaced expression, she knew that it wasn't a pack of lies, even if Bob had slightly embellished it. Her own daughter was a brazen hussy. But that didn't excuse her husband.

"I swear on what's dearest to me," said Bob, "that I went upstairs with the best intentions. I just wanted to give her a good spanking to punish her for having led me on by showing me her pussy. Well, instead of crying, she started to writhe and to show me her arse. That twisted girl couldn't get enough!"

Laura looked down. She was only too aware of the erotic effects of her husband's spankings. Bébé must have taken

after her in that respect. She felt guilty of having passed down a hereditary flaw.

Moreover, his voice had a truthful ring to it that she couldn't ignore. She could see that Bébé was only pretending to sniff. Earlier, when she had been on her knees in front of him, she hadn't looked as if she was being forced against her will. Laura remembered her daughter's gesture, how she expertly handled his big penis with both hands, and her hollowed cheeks as she sucked away. No, she decidedly hadn't looked as if she had been forced!

"I couldn't resist, dammit," he groaned pathetically, "I couldn't resist. Let he who hasn't given in to temptation cast the first stone. When she threw herself onto my cock, I could have stopped her, that's true. But, for God's sake, she had turned me on so much, I'm only human after all. I let her blow me since she enjoys it so much."

"Be quiet, Bob. That's enough now," yelled the pharmacist as she got up. "I've heard enough."

She was taken aback by the contempt that she felt towards her husband. From her daughter's silent indignation, she knew that that was not the whole truth. But she had made up her mind, she had to attend to the most urgent matters first.

"She'll almost certainly end up with a bun in the oven at this rate," cried Bob treacherously, "promiscuous as she is. AND THEN YOU'LL BE A GRANDMOTHER!"

That hit a nerve. Grandmother! And Laura who so wanted to pass for a young woman! Horrified by her step-father's scheming, Bébé understood that her fate was sealed. She made a pitiful effort to soften her mother.

"I'm still a virgin, Mum," she stammered, "you can check

if you like. They only do it to me from behind, there's no danger."

"From behind!"

It was too much. That 'from behind' was the last straw. Laura threw her arms in the air. She was at a loss. It was worse than anything she had anticipated. Her own daughter was being sodomised! Regaining her composure with great difficulty, the pharmacist showed her husband the door.

"Get out, Bob. Get out of my sight, you're a nasty piece of work. I want a divorce."

He went as white as a sheet. Bugger. He'd have to be a barman again, that job he detested. The late nights, the drunks, Christ, how bloody awful. Crushed, he turned on his heel.

"As for you, I'm sending you to boarding-school. I'll phone my niece Mimi. She's told me about a special institution where they put girls of your sort to protect them from themselves. A school where they teach them how to be good wives and cure them of their baser instincts. I know the headmistress by sight. She's a decent lady who seems very competent. We'll lock you up in there until you're old enough to be married off. You can pack tonight. Tomorrow, at dawn, I'll drive you there. I don't want a bastard in the family."

Understanding that nothing would make her mother change her mind, Bébé threw herself onto her bed and, with her face buried in her pillow, began to sob bitterly. She heard the door close... and the key turn in the lock. Her mother had locked her in her room for the night.

Chapter Eight: The pepper trick

Bob had been standing outside with his ear glued to the door and so hadn't missed a word that his wife had said. He told himself that if she sent the kid to boarding-school, he might have a chance of getting her to change her mind about the divorce. He knew Laura well; she had spoken in anger, but her flesh was weak and he had her by the pussy. He just needed to play his cards right. Once the little darling was out of the picture, Laura would no longer fear any competition and would be easier to mollify. Thinking hard, he ran downstairs.

The lounge was empty. The cards were still spread out on the table and the bottle of sloe gin had taken a bashing. Maybe Ernest had overdone it a bit; after all, he wasn't used to alcohol any more, after his long spell inside, and he'd probably gone upstairs to sleep it off. The kid was probably asleep as well. Strange that he hadn't gone to say goodnight to his sis. Maybe he'd heard what had happened?

Still chewing it over, Bob went to the kitchen. He had to act fast. He took the pepperpot from the spice rack, unscrewed the lid and tapped a pinch into his palm, before zipping across the hall to the couple's bedroom. There, he snorted the pepper as if it was a line of coke and immediately felt as if his brain was alight. With his sinuses on fire, he cursed under his breath and blew his nose hard. But too late, the pepper had penetrated his nasal membranes and his eyes were streaming. That had been the general idea, but he'd overdone it a tad. It was too much; he was crying like a baby. He hoped Laura wouldn't

smell a rat. Sobbing his heart out, he delved into the closet, pulled out his old cardboard suitcase from his barman days and threw it onto the bed. He then set about taking his clothes off the hangers.

~

Meanwhile, one floor above, Laura, who'd just locked her daughter in her room, hesitated on the landing. Perhaps it was dangerous to lock her in? What if there was a fire? She'd be trapped. She shrugged. And why on earth would there be a fire that very night? There was no way she was going to let that twisted child wander around freely after what she'd done. If a fire did break out, she'd just have to jump out of the window. Her room was only on the first floor, after all. She felt she had done the right thing and that she was partly vindicated for the appalling way she'd been treated. She approached the stairs. But the thought that a man who was just out of jail was staying under their roof stopped her in her tracks. You never know what's going through those men's minds. She had noticed the way Ernest slyly eyed up her daughter. She must have been blind not to notice until now the effect that little hypocrite had on men. It would be tempting fate to leave the key in the lock. Anyone could enter and do whatever he pleased with that budding nymphomaniac. Ernest, or even Bob for that matter. She knew that she was a heavy sleeper when she took her sleeping pills, and she would definitely take some tonight, otherwise, hyper as she was, she'd be in for a sleepless night. She retraced her steps and pocketed the key, then she went downstairs to tidy up, and when she'd finished, she entered her bedroom with a heavy heart.

The first thing she noticed was the battered suitcase, with its dull brass corners, on the bed. Bob, red-eyed and crying his heart out, was stuffing it with his summer clothes, which he'd pulled down from the top shelf. Mothballs had rolled onto the floor and he was glad of it, because their sickly stench covered up the smell of pepper that pervaded his person. Alarmed, Laura stared at her husband. It wasn't an act; he was really blubbing! She'd never seen him cry before. It shook her. She was filled with remorse and stammered, "Why are you crying, Bob? What's wrong?"

"Leave me alone! I'm crying with joy at the thought of getting out of here. I've had it up to here, you won't have to chuck me out, I'm going."

He had to play a close game. He carefully folded an old beige alpaca jacket and stuffed it into the case. A mothball fell out of the pocket and rolled out in front of him. He furiously crushed it underfoot.

"I'm going to call a cab," he thundered. "I won't stay a minute longer."

"Now, now, Bob, there's no screaming hurry. And anyway, you can't go just yet, what about your cousin?"

Bob pursed his lips magnanimously.

"OK," he conceded, "I'll stay tonight. But I'm leaving tomorrow."

"Come on, Bob, don't get yourself in such a state! We don't have to part on bad terms just because we're going to divorce. I'm not throwing you out. You can stay a few more days, until you sort yourself out."

"But earlier, you said 'tomorrow', didn't you? Did I hear correctly?"

"I said that because I was angry. It was just a figure of speech."

Red-eyed, Bob sniffed. He flopped onto the bed and looking disheartened, closed his suitcase. It was too full, so he couldn't get the lid down completely. Laura watched him struggling away; she was gobsmacked to see tears still rolling down his cheeks. Even though she was seeing it, she had trouble believing it. Perhaps, deep down, he really loved her, perhaps he had simply given in to carnal temptation? But just as she was beginning to feel dangerously sorry for him, she remembered the scene: her daughter on her knees and him, with his hands on his hips and a blissful look on his face. She'd seen that expression many times when she'd sucked him off.

Her rage was rekindled, mixed with a feeling of waste (to think they'd been so happy until tonight) and helplessness in the face of life's injustice. She burst into tears in her turn.

"Oh Bob, how could you do such a thing?" she wailed. "I trusted you so much. You can cry all you like, I'm not going to fall for your crocodile tears. Getting a blow-job from a kid! Don't you have any morals?"

He stretched his arms out towards her, in an imploring gesture that he'd seen some actor do in one of those cheesy TV soaps that Laura loved.

"I swear, Laura, I swear I didn't mean any harm! You've got to believe me!"

"Didn't mean any harm? A likely story! Oh, you can cry all right. Tomorrow I'm applying for a divorce. I'll send my daughter to boarding-school and I'll get a divorce. That way, I'll be rid of both of you."

At that thought, she cried even more, repeating, "Bob, Bob, how could you do such a thing?" She then threw herself down onto the bed and buried her face in the pillow. While she was sobbing away, Bob sidled up towards her on his buttocks.

"I'm weak, Laura, that's how," he whispered. "I'm not a bad guy, I'm just weak. I'm only human, dammit, I'm not a saint. She's your daughter after all, she looks like you. We'd drunk a lot of sloe gin, I didn't know what I was doing."

"Be quiet, please be quiet," shouted Laura, hugging her pillow. Despite his holier-than-thou attitude, Bob was letting his eyes wander thoughtfully over his wife's buxom behind. When she had thrown herself on the bed, her dress had ridden up mid-thigh. Her sobs were making her plump thighs wobble. He immediately had a hard-on. It always turned him on to hear a woman crying. He put a hand on Laura's hip.

"Stop it," he murmured, as he caressed her buttocks. "Don't cry, Laurette, you're breaking my heart."

Laura was so absorbed in her sorrow that she didn't react to this timid caress. Bob insidiously let his hand wander further down and his fingers crept into the cleft between her buttocks. He knew that that was where he would find the chink in her armour. If he could succeed in touching her arse, it was in the bag. As soon as her anus was being tickled, Laura no longer knew what she was doing.

"Laura, you've got to believe me," he murmured, edging nearer to the sensitive spot. "I was drunk, I lost my head. I didn't want to but I couldn't resist. When she started to provoke me..."

"That's right, are you accusing her of rape as well?"

"She didn't rape me, let's not exaggerate, but she did provoke me. I told you, throughout last summer, as soon as you were

out, she'd strip off. Cross my heart and hope to die. She was constantly shoving her tits in my face. And earlier, when I went upstairs to tell her that she could stop messing around, that her teasing wasn't working, that I would tell you everything about Jéréme, she did it again, but worse. She really went for it this time and lifted up her dress and showed me her arse, honest to God, saying, 'Don't you like my bum, Bob? Go on, give in to temptation, don't be so picky. Are you sure you don't want a piece of it as well? There's no reason why you shouldn't have some like the others. You'll see, it's so much better than my mother's!'"

"She said that? Ooh, the nasty little bitch, the little slut! Tomorrow, you mark my words, tomorrow she'll be packed off to that boarding-school. I've nursed a viper in my bosom."

"So, like a shot, I picked her up, threw her onto the bed and gave her a thorough spanking – you know what I'm like. Well, believe it or not, she loved it! Instead of crying, she was begging for more. 'Harder!' she kept yelling. 'Harder! Oh yes, Bob, hit me hard on the pussy, that's what I like best!'"

"Oh! Oh! But... but... but she's completely sick! Tomorrow, d'you hear, tomorrow..."

Deciding that it was time for action, Bob tactically moved his hand away from her sensitive zone and let it slide down Laura's thigh to the back of her knee; he then ran it up again, treacherously stroking her naked flesh.

"What are you doing, Bob?" she whined. "Stop stroking me, you bastard, now's not the time. Take your hand away, do you hear me?"

Bob did not heed these symbolic words of protest. With exquisite delicacy, he lifted Laura's dress above her loins, revealing her beautiful plump behind, which her knickers

didn't exactly conceal. This was because that evening, she was wearing a pair of those wisp-like black nylon knickers that he had bought for her at the sex shop and that he liked so much because they were see-through.

"Stop it, Bob. Don't do that... You're no longer entitled to."

"Er, excuse me, but I'd like to point out that we're still married. Until the divorce has been approved, I can do whatever I like! And by the way, if we divorce, who's going to take care of that beautiful big arse, eh? Can you tell me that? You'll never find anyone who'll take care of it as well as I do."

He tugged the knickers up her back to wedge them between her buttocks. When he did that, nothing would turn him on as much as to see the flesh bulge out from either side, knowing at the same time that her knickers were cutting her plump pussy and her clitoris in half at the front while sticking to her oozing flesh like a dressing to a wound. He saw her lifting her arse from the sensation so as to allow her knickers to penetrate her pussy. She sighed.

"Bob, be reasonable. Stop..."

But while with his other hand, he was cutting her pussy in two, he pulled one thigh away, and she let herself be moved.

"That's it, my lovely," said Bob encouragingly, "open up your fat bum. Oh, I love it so much, I've never seen one that turned me on as much as yours."

Bob sounded so sincere that Laura shuddered from head to toe. Even if he didn't love her, he loved to fuck her, she was sure of that. There were unmistakable signs. Bob delicately pulled her knickers out of her soaking cunt; he lifted them up, then pulled them aside to reveal her gaping pussy. It was so wet! Her knickers were soaked and there was already a stain on the bedspread. Holding her knickers with both hands, one

under his wife's stomach and the other between her buttocks, he put it back in the cleft and slowly started moving to and fro in a sawing motion.

"Bob," she begged, "stop, Bob, don't do that... Oh, that's not nice of you, you're taking advantage of my weakness."

"Open your pussy, darling, yes, like that."

He stopped his cello playing and slid a finger under the damp bow of the gusset, then ran it along the labia, into the sticky vulva, and finally thrust it deep into her vagina. Oh God! Laura bucked and arched her back like a cat on heat offering herself up to a tom. He removed his finger, moved up her pussy and pressed her clitoris. She squealed in spite of herself. His finger went back down, passed her vagina and teased her anus.

"Bob, stop! Oh, not there! Bob, you know that... Oh no, don't do that!"

His well-oiled finger was inexorably penetrating her arse. Moaning with ecstasy, Laura bit the pillow, ashamed of giving into her pleasure. That bastard was making a fool of her, she was putty in his hands. Bob removed his finger and sniffed her arse; he loved doing that.

"You smell like a randy whore," he murmured. "Yes, that's it, give all your little holes to your husband."

He put his finger back in her arse.

"Do you want a little suppository? It's good for your ailment. And then we can move on to more serious matters."

"No, Bob, I don't want to."

"Just the once, one last shag before we split up. For old times' sake."

He twisted his finger in her yielding anus as if he was scraping cream out of a jar. At the thought of their imminent separation, Laura, whose sobs had become more intermittent,

resumed shedding bitter tears. But even though she gave in to her sorrow, she cowardly didn't resist when Bob parted her thighs. When she felt the bedsprings give, she knew that he was between her legs and about to fuck her. With a heavy heart, she felt incapable of denying herself a good time any longer and lifted her behind to offer herself up to him.

"Yes, give it here," approved Bob, "that's right, open up your pussy, but try not to scream the house down when you come; no offence, but sometimes you really let go! Don't forget about my cousin in the attic room, where he can hear everything through the chimney flue. We mustn't wake him. He's very strait-laced, you know."

The head of his cock was nuzzling her pubic hair. Her flesh parted between his member like an over-ripe plum. He slowly sank into her gooey cunt. Christ, it was good! That dirty whore opened herself up, God, how open she was – he'd never felt a woman open herself as much and suck him inside so deeply. I'll give you divorce! He grabbed her buttocks and lifted her up before angrily plunging it in to the hilt. She moaned and bit the pillow. There, he was all the way in now, possessing her right up to the womb; it was in the bag. He started to pound away like a madman. She wanted a divorce? It wasn't that easy to divorce him, here, take this, and this, and this..! He'd teach her a lesson. Laura went wild, moaning and opening up, and gave herself to him. She was clawing and biting the pillow, drooling and writhing.

"Oh Bob," she gasped, "go easy on me, Bob, stop, please, you're driving me crazy, I won't be able to control myself! Please, Bob! If you carry on like this, I'll scream! Think of your cousin."

Her pleas fell on deaf ears. Bob was only heeding the rage

firing his balls (as if the pepper that he'd inhaled had found its way there) and was stabbing away at her faster and faster. He would pull out his cock soaked in her juices and ram it back in as if it were a death blow. The effect of this treatment was not long in coming. Laura began to scream at the top of her lungs as if he were murdering her. She no longer gave two hoots about Ernest's supposedly chaste ears! You should have heard her squeal!

"What a shame," thought Bob, "that I can't juggle these two women, and bugger the daughter by day and fuck the mother by night. Too late, I was stupid enough to get caught. I've blown it with the daughter, she's off to boarding-school tomorrow. But I've still got the mother. Shit, I've got to be careful that I don't lose both. I'll look after her. I'll make her forget this divorce nonsense."

He continued to hump her hard as if his life depended on it, which wasn't exactly incorrect. He didn't particularly care for the alternative, the drab nocturnal existence of a barman. He had had it up to there with drunks, whores and crawling home at dawn, unshaven and with eyes bloodshot from fatigue. Besides, in his own way, he loved his pharmacist; she was easy-going and generous, and she was terrific in bed. He would have had to be completely stupid to throw away such an opportunity.

"Can you feel it? Can you? Can you feel how it's pounding away at you?"

"Yes, Bob, I can feel it all right. You're the king, you bastard. Fuck me hard, ahhhha, ohhhhh... I'm dying, you swine, I'm going to have a heart attack!"

Concentrating now on his own pleasure, Bob closed his eyes and came. His spunk gushed deep inside her, probably

pulsing against her cervix judging from her shrieks from the depths of her stomach, as if she were in her death throes. She then immediately sobbed with relief.

"Oh Bob, that was so wonderful, darling! I hope your cousin didn't hear us. I'd be mortified."

He'd have to be as deaf as a post not to hear anything! This time, Bob patted himself on the back as he pulled out.

"I think I scored full marks there," he thought. "By the skin of my teeth, but I reckon I've come through the other end. I'm out of the woods now."

He felt quite smug and, chuckling, patted her bottom in a proprietorial manner. But that was a fatal mistake!

"You think this is funny, do you?" cried Laura, seething with a rage that took him aback. "So you think that you can just fuck me well and I'll be under your thumb? You bastard! You rat! You shit!"

She got so carried away in her fury that she knocked him back onto his suitcase and started to pummel his chest. She was beating him like a drum, and he sounded like one as well.

"You swine! You turd! You get sucked off by the daughter, then you fuck the mother! You crooked bastard! You probably thought all you had to do was stick it inside me and I'd change my mind. Well, I'll show you!"

Screaming like a banshee, she unbuttoned his fly as Bob lay there, utterly flabbergasted (he'd never seen her like this before). She ripped off his clothes as if she was skinning a rabbit and suddenly he was naked. He was too dumbfounded to react and watched her, open-mouthed. However, when he saw her pull his mock-croc belt off his trousers and wrap around her wrist he realised what she was about to do. Hold

your horses! There must be some mistake, love! But too late, the belt started to lash at his thighs, just beneath his nuts. He leapt up in shame, like a carp that's just been flung onto the river bank, but she kicked him full on the chest, like a mule, and he went rolling head over heels over his stupid bloody suitcase. The belt caught him right on the buttocks, filling him with stinging wonderment. He had never felt so stunned in his life. Schlack, schlack, schlack! The leather strap stung him with unbelievable cruelty at least ten times. "Christ," he thought, "is that what they feel when they're being flogged? I understand everything now."

"Bastard! Bastard! Take that, you crook!" gasped Laura, who was unrecognisable from anger. She was nevertheless astonished to see that he was still quite passive. He was lying on his stomach, with his arms outstretched, and at each blow he would tense his buttocks by arching his back a little. Something suddenly occurred to her and kneeling on the bed, she slid one hand under her husband's thighs. She lifted his balls and felt higher up. Her fingers closed on a huge erection.

"You're hard, you sicko, does this turn you on?"

Bob lifted his body so that she could get a better grip. She hesitated then held his rod again and exposed the big clammy head.

"You dirty sod, you animal, being beaten with a belt works for you, eh?"

She teased his glans between her thumb and forefinger and saw Bob's anus tighten. He was even more surprised than she was by his reaction. It was definitely a day for discoveries. She started to wank him very gently.

"You filthy beast," she repeated in a hushed voice. "You're no better than my daughter. Look at that, you should be ashamed."

She rolled him over and he immediately opened his thighs to show her everything. His cock was as hard as a rock and the glans, swollen with blood, was so red that it was almost purple.

"It's so hard, Bob! Just look at that!" The glans was so swollen that she found it difficult to cover it with the foreskin and then pull it back again. It glowed like a bulb.

"Oh, you naughty boy!" whispered Laura in memory of one of the incestuous games they used to play when they were newlyweds. "Have you seen the state of you? You're a disgrace! Let Mummy have a look…"

Bob quivered and frantically watched as she crawled on her knees to get nearer to him. Wild-eyed, she opened her mouth. She greedily engulfed it with her mouth, taking it in as far as it would go, but he was so hard that she couldn't get it all in. Bob groaned with pleasure. He felt buoyed by a nameless ecstasy, as if his body was peeling off the bed and hovering in thin air like that of a levitating fakir. While she sucked him voraciously, Laura was moaning, crazed by the orgasm which was taking hold of her. She was wild with anticipation, on the verge of a crying fit, so intense did it feel. No, she definitely would never be able to do without a man like him. His cock was so big and so hard! It was so lovely to have it in her mouth. And not just in her mouth… Suddenly, she impatiently stopped sucking and straddled him. She crouched above his member in an obscene position, as if she was about to piss on him, and impaled herself. It looked like a huge bone! Maybe he was a bastard, she repeated to herself, a right shit, a perv, a sicko, and he'd made her even more twisted than him, but the harm was done now, she might as well make the most of it, because now that she was rotten to the core like him, she would never

be able to live without him. It would be suicide, worse, *la petite mort*. She cried hoarsely as she rammed it in to the hilt and sat on her husband's balls which looked like two little elastic cushions.

"In the arse," pleaded Bob with a strange voice. "In the arse, darling, please!"

He was begging her! Whatever next? She continued for a couple of thrusts, moaning in ecstasy.

"You think so?" she panted. "D'you think it would be better?"

"Yes, yes, quickly, put it in your arse."

His eyes were popping out of his head. What she didn't know was that he was fantasising about Bébé. He thought it would be easier to imagine that he was buggering the daughter, knowing that she was a virgin, than when he was fucking the mother.

Laura, who was light years away from thinking up such convoluted schemes, lifted herself up to let out his bone. She then positioned her anus above his cock which she held like a candle. She always felt deliciously filthy when she was buggered in that position, with her pussy wide open and facing Bob who could play with her. When it entered her, she felt as if she was doing a poo, but in reverse; it filled her bowels, far into her rectum.

Up and down she went, like a merry-go-round horse bobbing on its pole, and she thought of her customers. If they could only see her now, the respectable pharmacist who was so strait-laced! The old gentleman who had rheumatism, for example, or the sales rep for those Carter liver pills, whatever would they think?

Bob wailed strangely, like a baby, and leaned back, arching

his back, and she knew that he was about to come and quickly engulfed him, crushing his balls under her buttocks. It was like a geyser in her arse and she squealed. She loved it so much when it sprayed her in bursts. After the final spasm, exhausted by the excesses of his orgasm, Bob lay back, hitting with his neck the open suitcase, and promptly fell asleep. He would often fall asleep after shooting his load. Laura couldn't get used to it. She would have preferred a cuddle after abandoning herself to him, but he'd just snore it off. She thought that he could have made an effort that night and lifted herself up to remove his cock from her arse. She was relieved to see that she hadn't soiled it and feeling sorry for him, she dragged him up by the armpits and lifted him so as to move the case that was probably digging into him. Christ, he was heavy! She moved closer so as to shift him. He was her man, he was all hers. After she'd managed to wedge a pillow under his head, she kissed him softly on the lips. This didn't stop him snoring. Suddenly intrigued, she wrinkled her nose; what was that smell? It couldn't be his aftershave that smelt so strong. It was so spicy, it almost made her cry. Made her cry? Puzzled, she sniffed his mouth, then his nostrils. For Christ's sake! He stank of pepper!

Suddenly, everything became clear. That was the reason behind those lovely tragic tears which had intrigued her earlier. The bastard! What a shit he was! He'd carried it off brilliantly.

"You beast! You swine! So you think you're going to get away with this? We'll see about that! D'you hear me, Bob? I'm dead serious, you know!"

She shook him but to no avail. When he was asleep, he was dead to the world.

"The bastard's snoring! That's all he ever does! His

lordship's got his end away and now he's out like a light. And what about me? How am I going to sleep with this din in the background?"

Bob's snores were far from discreet. Even earplugs wouldn't have been sufficient to muffle them.

"I'll have to take my little pills again... Otherwise, I'll be up all night."

She pulled open the bedside table drawer. She was so exasperated that she was muttering to herself, as if she was in a play.

"I'll take a Tranxene and a Temesta. A yellow one, they're stronger. I'm too anxious. I could kill him when he snores like that. And I'll take a Valium as well for good measure."

Being a pharmacist, she could just help herself, there was no need for a prescription. A pharmacist who indulges in tranquillisers is even worse than a baker who likes cakes.

"If I don't get to sleep with all that, I give up."

She hesitated. Tonight, she really needed a strong dose. She added a little blue pill of Rohypnol. Drugged up as she was now, there was no way she'd stay awake. A bomb wouldn't wake her.

CHAPTER NINE:
A NON-VIOLENT BREAKING AND ENTERING

Lying on his bed, Ernest was listening to the voices emanating from the fireplace. Owing to an unusual acoustic arrangement, he could hear everything that was happening two floors below as clearly as if he'd switched on the radio. Laura's shrieks had roused him from a deep sleep and at first he had wondered where this racket was coming from. He had sat bolt upright and felt struck by nausea. Bloody hell, that was some hangover! He should have gone easy on the sloe gin. You drink it like water and then it really hits you. He couldn't even recall getting into bed. He had hit the hay fully dressed without even taking off his shoes. While Laura was squealing like a cat on heat, he gingerly touched his temples. It felt as if there was a steel vice around his skull. Moans and groans were coming from the hearth. Despite his ghastly hangover, he couldn't help chuckling to himself. Well, well, if it wasn't his cousin banging the missus! And, my Godfathers, it certainly sounded like they're having a whale of a time!

Beaming despite his thumping headache, he went over to the fireplace and lifted the flue-shutter so as to hear better. It was as if he'd turned up the volume on the radio. He could even hear the squeaking bedsprings. His cousin was really going at it hammer and tongs, no wonder the poor bitch was yelling her head off, he must be giving her cervix a right bashing. Whatever happened to discretion, love? He was titillated as he remembered the pharmacist's shapely big arse; Ernest would have had two words in particular to say to that arse.

Damn, he was hard now. He touched his dick and hesitated. No, he wouldn't have a wank. He had better things to do. Now that the pharmacist had come, it had gone quiet. Ernest couldn't hear what they were saying. He shrugged. His mind was wandering. He was slowly sobering up. Social rehabilitation. Social rehabilitation! That's why he'd got so smashed earlier. That stupid bitch kept banging on about her nephew who was a lawyer and an expert in these matters. "He'll definitely find you an interesting job, he has a lot of contacts."

A lot of contacts. You bet. Ernest wasn't too keen on social rehabilitation. He'd been there, done that. He knew what it meant. Window-cleaner, night-watchman, khazi-unblocker. No thanks. He hadn't got out of jail to work like a slave. He had better ideas. He got up, had a slash in the washbasin, let the water run for a bit and gave his face a quick wash. His thoughts were becoming clearer; the vice was loosening around his skull. A decision gradually took shape in his addled brain.

First of all, he would still go and see the nephew who was a lawyer. It couldn't do any harm and it might be interesting. Otherwise, he'd be off to Brazil. But for that, he needed some dosh. And he knew where to get it. A pharmacist as posh as his cousin's wife had to have some readies. She probably had a safe in her bedroom; she was a middle-class provincial woman who was getting on a bit, she was bound to have a safe hidden behind a painting. He'd go and make a large dent in that safe. It wouldn't take a minute. He grabbed his tool kit; it was an elegant leather toolbag that looked more like a doctor's medical case. It did in fact contain a stethoscope, which does come in quite handy to crack safes. Ernest put it around his neck and went over to the fireplace to listen. The voices had died down. All he could hear from the hearth was loud regular snoring.

Now that he'd got his leg over, his cousin was getting some shut-eye; classic! Barefoot, with his stethoscope bouncing on his chest and his toolbag in his hand, Ernest went down to the next floor. He passed the little sweetheart's door with a twinge of regret. What a little slut with her gorgeous tits and her big cocksucker's mouth; he would have enjoyed a chinwag with her, but all in good time. First he had to deal with that safe. The old how's-your-father would have to wait. He continued down to the ground floor. The married couple's bedroom was at the end of the corridor. He approached without making a sound and pricked up his ears.

He put his hand on the doorknob, turned it slowly and pushed open the door. Before he even noticed that the room was still dimly lit by the nightlight, he felt his cock stiffen, as if it anticipated what they, namely his cock and Ernest, were about to witness. He froze. The pharmacist was standing with her back to him, bent over the bedside table. Ernest stopped breathing. Christ, what an arse! She was wearing just a diaphanous nightie which skimmed her bum. And because she was standing in front of the bedside lamp, which made the flimsy nylon garment transparent, he could get a good eyeful. Ernest loved those big soft arses with slightly sagging buttocks. The pharmacist's ample behind corresponded perfectly to his most demanding preferences.

The door was merely ajar, barely a crack, and the corridor was plunged in darkness. The pharmacist would therefore not have noticed him, even if she had been facing him. She was muttering to herself and scratching her arse.

"I'll have to put some Vaseline on. He's opened me up too much. What a bastard. I'm really cut up about it. Nasty brute. I catch him getting a blow-job from my daughter, he blames

her, I decide to send her to boarding-school to protect her from herself and I tell him I want a divorce, which is perfectly understandable under the circumstances. And what does he do? He snorts some pepper and buggers me like a cheap tart. And then he snores. And I take it! I must have a screw loose, no doubt about it."

She had lifted up her nightie and was feeling her anus.

"Though I have to admit that that bastard really made me come. Listen to him snoring."

Ernest was admiring the beautiful behind that she was showing off to him, but his mind was racing. So his swine of a cousin was screwing the daughter, and the mother had just found out! She turned round and he saw that she was holding a tube of pills in her hand. He immediately recognised it. In jail, they would often be given sleeping pills to knock them out. Rohypnol. That's why she seemed so out of it.

"I've already had one. And a Temesta. And a Valium as well, I think. It wouldn't be wise..."

He couldn't believe his ears. That was already enough to put an elephant to sleep and she wanted to take another? Go on then, he encouraged her in thought, that way I can deal with that safe in peace. He watched her pop the blue pill into her mouth and wash it down with some water. She sat on the bed and folded a leg to slide it under the sheet next to Bob who was snoring his head off. Ernest gulped. Amongst her tousled pubic hair, he could make out the pinkish flesh of her pussy gaping lasciviously. The last pill had really bludgeoned an already groggy Laura and she leaned back and brought up her other leg into the bed. She pulled the quilt up to her chin and, forgetting the night-light, she crashed out.

Ernest was familiar with the effects of the crap she'd just

swallowed. It would knock you out for three hours as if you'd been hit with a sledgehammer, then you'd wake up completely woozy and you'd have to take another. He waited five minutes then entered and approached the bed. She was sleeping like an Egyptian mummy, totally still. Holding his case like a doctor, he leaned over her and looked at her thoughtfully.

"Go and see to that safe, you fool," hissed a voice deep inside him. "Leave that crazy bitch to sleep."

The voice was certainly right, there was no doubt about that, but he hadn't seen a fanny in seven years. He lifted the quilt and threw it back onto his cousin who was sleeping on his front with his arms outstretched, like a soldier who'd been shot in the heart. When he had uncovered Laura's body, he leant over to smell her. The scent of woman filled his nostrils and he had to unzip his fly because his cock was bursting out. He popped out the glans and gave it a squeeze between his thumb and forefinger. He looked down at her crotch, the triangle of hair and the tip of the cleft. What a shame she hadn't fallen asleep with her legs open. To console himself for not being able to see everything, he sniffed her pubic hair, he was so close that the hairs tickled his nose, filling his nostrils with her smell. It was the fragrance of a woman who has come, at once pungent and sweet, in addition to the spiciness of sweat. He almost came there and then. Seven years is a long time! He was about to leap on her when, at the very last minute, he managed to regain his composure. He froze like a pointer. He could see her big tits with their broad nipples through the pink nylon. He made an effort to straighten up, drenched in sweat, and resolutely turning his back on temptation, he made a bee-line for a hideous seascape, an eyesore on the facing wall, above a little cherrywood desk.

His hunch had been correct. The safe was indeed hidden behind this daub. The painting swung round on its hinges. God, those middle-class people were as thick as planks! They'd always go for the most obvious hiding places. They thought they were being really clever by stashing their safes away behind paintings, but it was the first place he would look. And talk about a safe, it was a real tin can. It looked as if it dated back to the First World War, it probably belonged to her grandfather. You could open it in three minutes flat. Wanna bet? Three minutes, no more, no less. With a toothpick and a nail file. He pouted in disgust, placed his superfluous toolbag on the desk and stuffed the ends of the stethoscope into his ears. His cousin's snores abated. He placed the suction disc of the instrument onto the safe and started to twiddle the knobs to find out the combination. Click... click... click... a harder click... click... click... click... another one. He chuckled to himself. A child could have done it. The reinforced door swung open and he started his inventory.

Letters. They always have letters in their safes. He shook his head in disbelief at such stupidity. Premium bonds. Shares. All this was of no use to him, he didn't bother with this stuff. Too complicated. And what was this? He couldn't believe his eyes. Some Russian bonds as old as the hills, as big as primary school certificates. Honestly, you've got to laugh. They sell that sort of rubbish a penny a sheet in flea markets to people who collect old paper. Ah, here we go. There were some greenbacks right at the bottom. Wow! They were brand new, still crisp. They smelled of ink. Amazed, he put the wads on the desk. There was at least a hundred grand there. He could feel the cold sweat trickling down his back.

He turned round. The pharmacist was still asleep, lying

perfectly still. Her thighs were slightly apart. He could glimpse some pink flesh, a vertical slit between the fleece. No, it wouldn't be wise. He'd just done a seven-year stretch. Now wasn't the time to slip up. He knew where the money was and that was all that mattered. It was best to leave it where it was safe. He'd come back for it when he needed it. Tomorrow, he'd go and see that lawyer; he'd keep a low profile for a while and he'd accept any shitty job they offered him, even if it was potato-peeler in a boarding-school. They called that 'kitchen hand'. And later, when everyone had forgotten about him, he'd come back for the dough and bye bye everyone. He'd be off to Brazil! He put back the Russian bonds, the shares, the love letters and the wads of cash, except one, which he stuffed into his pocket, one for the road as it were. He closed the safe, scrambled the combination, which he didn't even bother to memorise, and swung the painting back onto it.

Clutching his toolbag, he returned to the bed. He had just remembered a murderer with whom he had shared a cell for two years. He was well-built but of a nervous disposition and so Rohypnol would keep him going. There were four of them in that cell and as soon as the guy had taken his blue pill, he'd pass out as Laura had done. And so, one after the other, the three other lads would bugger him. He had never noticed a thing. He constantly had to go to the hospital wing because he'd got piles from all the sodomy. But he'd never woken up in the middle of it.

Whistling under his breath, Ernest put his bag on the floor. He grabbed hold of the hem of the nightie and pulled the flimsy garment under the buxom buttocks of the sleeping woman, then he hitched it up completely, freeing the breasts, which rolled gently, dewy with sweat, over her chest. Christ, a

naked woman, and she was all his! A real one, made of flesh and blood, with her smells, her hairs, a hole, everything he needed to be happy. To think that he'd only seen photos of women during those seven years, old copies of *Penthouse* spattered with dried spunk and which they'd have to buy off the screws for a small fortune. He stared at the scene before his eyes. The night-light bathed her radiant skin in a soft pink glow. Laura had made herself more comfortable and her thighs were no longer clenched. He could almost see her entire pussy. The moist cleft was gaping and the pink undulating flesh bulged out between the labia lined with dark fur.

"I've got to touch her, looking isn't enough. I'll touch everything, she won't notice a thing."

His prick stuck out in front of him, twitching spasmodically, and drew him irresistibly towards Laura like a dog tugging at his master's leash to sniff a turd. He leaned over her and put his stethoscope between her breasts. Her heartbeat was slow and regular, as was her breathing. She was sound asleep. He let go of the stethoscope and crouched by the bed. He placed his hands on the flesh of her chest, just under her breasts. Laura sighed and her nipples immediately stiffened. Goodness, she was quick off the mark! He couldn't wait any longer and grabbed her boobs. They were warm, soft and springy. He started to tremble with joy. Her nipples were poking up like two little horns. He moved his face forward, stuck out his tongue and licked the big brown disc that encircled the nearest nipple. Oh God, it was good! He put the whole nipple in his mouth, sucked on it, nibbled it.

"Oh Bob," sighed Laura, "you bastard." She slurred her speech like a drunk. The guy they used to bugger would sometimes speak like that while they were at it, but he wasn't

really conscious. Ernest moved to the other nipple. The sour taste of sweat gradually gave way to the taste of female flesh, that indescribable and fascinating blandness. He alternated from one tit to the other, sucking voraciously and greedily. From time to time, he would stop sucking and teased her nipples with his fingers. She stuck out her chest to proffer herself better and imperceptibly opened her thighs. The smell of sex became gradually overpowering. The slut was getting horny in her sleep. She got wet easily. He couldn't bear it any longer and moved lower to see what was happening down below. He unceremoniously grabbed her knees and pushed her legs apart. The slit of her pussy widened like a corolla and a dribble of moisture oozed from her vagina. He brought his nose closer to the hole and inhaled its perfume. He loved women with a pungent pussy like hers.

"Bob, Bob, you bastard, why d'you do that, eh?"

With his fingertips, Ernest parted the tacky labia surrounding the vulva. Everything opened up. It was so totally different to the pussies he would draw in biro between the buttocks of the queers he had to fuck in the nick. This was the real McCoy. So as to admire it better, he grabbed a pillow and stuffed it under her buttocks. She was snoring, knocked out by those pills. He opened up her whole bag of tricks and fell into a mesmerised contemplation. Bloody hell, how he loved to admire a gaping pussy! He couldn't explain it. Perhaps he was abnormal, most guys weren't so keen on them, or so they said. They even found it a bit gross, it was too slimy. It was just something you put your cock into and emptied your balls. But Ernest would delight in finding a lovely plump, ripe cunt like the pharmacist's. He had the impression that his life had not been in vain.

The dribbling pink flesh unfurled like an accordion between the hairs glistening with threads of goo like a spider's web. And the hole opened up like a silently imploring mouth. Ernest was fascinated by this fragile flesh, it looked like lace. He sniffed the clit and gently licked it. He sucked it and felt the tiny tongue of flesh quiver in his mouth. His angular chin wallowed in the warm wetness and dug a crater in the vagina that was drawing him in like a plunger. He would have wanted to push his head inside, just to see what it looked like.

"Oh Bob, Bob... are you sucking my clit, Bob? You're sucking it well!"

He felt as happy as when he succeeded in opening a safe. He was breaking into a woman's body. It drove him wild. He leaned back, his mouth all sticky.

"I've got to fuck her. She won't wake up, she's too dopey. And if she does wake up, she'll think she was dreaming, or that it's her bloke. I just have to have her."

He couldn't pass up on such a lovely oozing pussy. There's nothing doing, it's in a different league to a boy's arse. He positioned himself between Laura's thighs. Guiding it in with one hand, he opened her cunt with his cock while propping himself up on the pillow that he'd wedged under her arse to lift her up. When he felt the warm softness of the vagina greedily engulfing him, he thought he was going to pass out. He hadn't screwed a woman for seven years! He gradually gave in to her smooth suction pipe. There was no need to thrust it in, it just found its way in. She was so hot inside and she anticipated his movements. She was babbling incoherently in her altered chemical state.

"Bob, stop, yes... no... oh, Bob, you bastard, fuck me hard, hard!"

She didn't have to ask twice. He entered her fully as easily as if his penis was made of lead, right up to the hilt, and he felt as if he were drowning. He had no intention of drawing it out and felt his orgasm welling up from deep down, from his very marrow, or even deeper still, deeper than time immemorial, and he spurted copiously, leaving him frantic, panting and practically dead. Slumped on top of her, he was crushing her under his weight and his balls were still emptying themselves jerkily, causing them both to moan in ecstasy.

"Oh Bob, Bob... I've never felt that with anyone else... Oh, you really know how to fuck me, Bob, you're the one... you're the one... Oh, my love..."

Yeah, yeah, thought Ernest. He lay on top of her like a dead fish. She had come in her sleep, he had distinctly felt her pussy clench around his cock. And now, he was wallowing in the soft and moist gooeyness of her vagina and felt as if he were dying.

An hour later, he felt unpleasantly cold and woke up with a start. His penis had almost completely slipped out of her, semen was dribbling from her vagina and it had dried on his balls, matting his pubes. God, he'd very nearly messed up; all three of them could have woken up together in the married couple's bed.

Ernest pulled out of her warm vagina and stood up. Stunned, he stared at the woman he'd just fucked; she was still snoring with her pussy gaping and semen trickling between her buttocks. He hoped he hadn't got her pregnant. That would be funny. He could be the godfather! No, she was bound to be

on the pill; she was a pharmacist after all! He sniggered, tugged the pillow from under her buttocks, rolled the nightie over her, covered her with the quilt and switched off the bedside lamp. Then he picked up his Dr Kildare bag and left the room.

"I feel so much better now," he thought as he climbed the stairs. He felt very perky at the thought of having emptied himself into the intended receptacle instead of his hand or some poofter's arse. He would sleep soundly now.

He laughed like a drain at the thought that tomorrow morning, he and the pharmacist would see each other again over breakfast and she wouldn't have a clue that he'd screwed her during the night.

Chapter Ten:
Doctor Kildare does his rounds

As he reached the first-floor landing, Ernest saw his reflection walking towards him in the large mirror behind the hat-stand. He looked just like Dr Kildare with his case and his stethoscope round his neck. He waved at himself and his reflection waved back. With a graceful little hop, he was about to climb the next flight when a twitch in his groin made him stop in front of Bébé's door.

"Now what?" he said to his dick, which was tugging him towards the door. "No way, old boy, we're turning in now."

But his cock was stronger-willed than he was. It was always the way, it always had the last word. In a flashback, he recalled the big, hypocritical and falsely innocent eyes of that little cock-sucker, and her big soft mouth with its corners turned downwards into a perpetual pout.

He also remembered what he had heard coming from downstairs. After all, if she had sucked off her cousin, there was no reason why he shouldn't partake as well. Why shouldn't he go and play doctors and nurses with her? He turned the doorknob without thinking and pushed the door. But it was locked. Damn. He peered through the keyhole. No key on the other side. Heavens, they'd locked her in! That got him thinking. Why had she been locked in? He had to find out. He opened his toolbag, fished out his oilcan and his set of picklocks. He dribbled some paraffin into the keyhole and chose a picklock. The oiled lock, handled carefully, clicked open very easily. He entered. The curtains weren't drawn and

thanks to the glow from the starry sky, he was able to make out the bed in the corner of the room and a pale shape on the pillow. His eyes became accustomed to the darkness and he could see the bedside lamp. He picked it up, put it on the floor so that it would not dazzle Bébé, and switched it on.

She was asleep with her face towards him, her hair in front of her eyes and her thumb in her mouth. He was struck by the odd position of her body. Her knees were bent and lifted the duvet like a tent. She was lying on her back, with her legs apart and her head to one side. Judging from her position, he suspected that she'd masturbated and that she'd dozed off without straightening her legs. He gently took her hand and removed her thumb from her mouth. He replaced it with his own which she immediately began to suck. He feverishly unbuttoned his fly, freed his cock which still smelt of his come and her mother's juices, and stuffed the head between her lips. She sucked away at it, even more greedily than before, as if the taste had aroused some sort of reflex in her.

With trembling knees, Ernest arched his back to push his cock into her mouth. She hollowed her cheeks and he felt her tongue gently swirl around it. He stood very still, savouring this amazing sensation. Her soft warm mouth suckled him like a big ravenous newborn. He carefully lifted the duvet and uncovered her knees. He got quite a shock when he saw her wide open pink pussy, surrounded with fine hairs. Her hand was still on it with her fingers in the slit. He was right, she had fallen asleep while wanking. He lifted her hand and leaned over to sniff her cunt and arse. Bloody hell, she smelt even more delicious than her mother! He mustn't wake her too soon, she could get scared and start yelling. He pulled the duvet back up, pulled his cock out of her mouth, took her

hand and stuffed her thumb back into her mouth, but he did all this extremely slowly, like a zombie. When he had finished, he took a deep breath and put the bedside lamp back on the table so that the light fell onto her face. He saw her screw up her face. Her eyes opened and she stared at him. He didn't expect her to wake up so quickly. She took her thumb out of her mouth.

"What are you doing in my room?" She didn't seem the slightest bit alarmed. "The door was locked, how did you get in?"

He tried to bluff, but he was a little intimidated by the silly goose's composure.

"Don't forget I have nimble fingers. Weren't you listening to my cousin at dinner? No lock has ever resisted me, they all give in to my gypsy charm."

Bébé frowned and looked distrustful. There was a funny taste in her mouth. He saw her lick her lips and understand. She suddenly blushed, she had recognised the taste.

"Have you been here long?"

"I've just come in. You're a really light sleeper, you know."

She sat up and stared at him. Because he was holding his case in front of him, she couldn't see that he had forgotten to do up his fly. At the foot of the bed, there was a chair with a pair of tights and a pair of knickers hanging off the back. He pulled it towards him and sat down. He took his packet of Camels out of his pocket. He lit one, took a drag and handed it to her like a peace offering.

"Want a drag?" She took the cigarette and inhaled. The taste of tobacco made her forget about the other taste.

"What do you want from me?"

"I just wanted to say goodnight, we didn't have a chance

to talk earlier. And I heard stuff. Sounds like you've got a problem with my cousin."

He deliberately lied so as to find out the truth.

"He was complaining to your mother that you jump on him whenever you get a chance."

Bébé's eyes widened indignantly.

"What a bastard! He's the one who jumped on me! He threatened to tell my mother everything about what I get up to with my brother... and..."

Shit! She'd given herself away again! What was wrong with her? Ernest could tell that she regretted divulging too much and came to her assistance.

"With your brother? So what? Big deal! As if it was anything to get worked up about! It's normal, when you've got a brother, you've got to make the most of it. All sisters behave like you. When I was little, I started with my older sisters. That's how you learn. Then I taught my little sisters. It's the same in every family."

She couldn't tell whether he was winding her up or not. That guy was a real clown, it was impossible to know what he was really thinking.

"And anyway," continued Ernest, "if you do it with your brother, it stays in the family. It's better to do it with him than with a stranger. That way, you're sure you won't catch anything. Is that why your mother's packing you off to boarding-school? She's really reactionary!"

Bébé shook her head.

"No, it's not because of that. She doesn't know about Bertrand. Bob didn't tell her. It's because she caught Bob and me while I was..." She blushed; she just couldn't say it. She slowly straightened her legs under the duvet.

"Oh yes, I heard about that; you were giving him a blow-job."

She started.

"Did he tell you?"

Ernest sniggered.

"No, a little bird told me. So that swine betrayed you to clear his name. What a tosser! He's really disgusting. In prison, there were guys like him who'd suck up to the screws and shop their mates just to be in the screws' good books. It was sickening."

Bébé looked at him without saying a word. This guy was a real character! She forgot to hold up the duvet, which slipped down to her waist. Her nipples showed through her nightie.

"They're cute, aren't they?" whispered Ernest, pointing at them. "You don't fancy showing me your gorgeous tits?"

What a clown! Bébé couldn't help giggling. She hesitated to pull up the duvet, was about to and then gave up with a shrug. The con's gaze tickled her nipples. He was quite a funny bloke really. She knew perfectly well why he'd come into her room. It wasn't astrophysics. She thought of her blissfully unaware sleeping mother. Something stirred in her flesh.

"I haven't seen a pretty pair of tits in seven years, except in magazines. Show me yours, there's a good girl! I promise I won't touch them."

"You cheeky sod! And why on earth would I show them to you? And anyway, you can see them as it is, this thing's transparent."

She coquettishly stuck out her chest, while watching him closely.

"It's not the same through the fabric... It's better naked, it's more natural. Go on, be a dear. And anyway, you're going off to boarding-school. You, who likes boys so much, you'll have to do without for a while. Why don't we do something that we both enjoy?"

She shrugged but didn't answer. She was feeling warm between her legs.

"Your nipples are poking out," whispered Ernest, leaning over to admire them. "See that? They're lifting up the nylon."

She looked down. Ernest put forward his index finger and caressed one of her nipples through the fabric. She shuddered and stared at it. He carefully cupped a breast.

"Take your hand away or I'll scream!"

He quickly removed his hand. He felt a little crestfallen, but then heard her chortle. He couldn't work her out at all.

"I bet I gave you a fright there." She licked her lips. "I wouldn't have screamed, I'm not that sort of girl."

"What sort are you then?"

She didn't answer. As if he needed to ask!

"You're going to be a big hit in boarding-school. All the prefects will be fighting over you. They're all dykes in boarding-schools. It's like the women who work in women's prisons. Have you ever done it with a girl?"

Caught off guard, Bébé shook her head. No, she'd never done it with a girl. What with all the boys that she had at her disposal, why on earth would she have tried it with a girl? And do what, exactly? She frowned. She was genuinely puzzled.

"Done what? What can you do with a girl?"

"What do you do with boys? You suck them off, don't you? Well, with girls it's the same thing. You'd lick each other's pussies. It's like in the nick, we used to bugger each other for want of women. But we weren't poofs for all that!"

He could see a dreamy glint in her eyes. She had often been licked by boys; she enjoyed it. She wondered what it would be like to go down on a girl. Ernest moved his chair closer and grabbed one of her tits again. She had told him that she

wouldn't scream, so why not? He felt its weight and fingered it. It was wonderful. With his thumb, he stroked the pointing nipple. Bébé's nostrils quivered, she looked up at him from beneath her hair that was in front of her eyes. He tweaked the nipple and she parted her lips.

"Do you at least know how to give good blow-jobs?" asked Ernest huskily.

The Camel that he'd lit had burnt down. He pinched it out like a con. Bébé seemed impressed.

"Don't you burn your fingers when you do that?"

"No, I'm used to it. Fag ends don't burn me. What's burning me now, and not just my fingers, is your nipple."

Again, she giggled stupidly, and it was such a turn-on. He rolled her springy nipple between his thumb and forefinger.

"You didn't answer me. Do you suck them off properly?"

"Well, they've never complained," giggled Bébé. The little tart!

"And what about grown-ups? Do you suck them off properly as well? I don't mean Bob, of course. I bet you're good at it, I can tell just from looking at your mouth, it's a cock-sucker's mouth, a glutton's mouth."

He let his toolbag slide off his lap and his penis popped up from his open fly like a jack-in-the-box. Bébé stared when she saw the scarlet glans emerging from the foreskin.

"Do you like my trouser snake?" asked Ernest, standing up and thrusting it in her face.

Bébé pouted. It wasn't as big as Bob's, but it was still respectable. It was certainly much larger than Jéréme's or even Émile's. And the glans was oddly shaped, a little flat.

"In prison, I used to stick it up boys' arses, but don't worry, I washed it earlier."

What he didn't mention was that he'd washed it in her mouth. He moved closer and because she didn't back away, she had to squint to look at the fat glans that was twitching in front of her nose.

"Take it in your little hand, there's a good girl," he begged. "Don't be afraid, it won't bite."

She shook her head and pouted even more.

"Whatever next? Who do you take me for? Put it away, you should be ashamed of yourself!"

He didn't fall for this offended nonsense. She just wanted to play hard to get, for the sake of form. He was familiar with her sort of slut, it makes them wet to know that they're keeping you on tenterhooks.

"Look at my lovely bollocks," he said to tempt her. He cupped them in his hand. "They're bursting. And yet, I've just emptied them inside your mother, but I've got a lot stored up."

"My mother? You're joking, right? My mother's asleep; she's probably taken her pills..."

"Exactly. She didn't notice a thing. And that pillock snoring next to her didn't hear a thing either."

Dumbfounded, Bébé looked up at him. Something told her that he wasn't lying. She shivered. She was frightened all of a sudden, he wasn't as funny any more. But at the same time, this fear felt nice and it made her open and wet.

"You did that?"

"As sure as I'm standing here. Come on, suck it, please..."

He stroked her head and pulled her neck towards him.

"Let go of me. I don't mind doing it, but I don't want you to force me."

He took his hand away and pushed his cock forward. The head touched her lips. He had the feeling that she was trying

not to laugh. He rubbed his cock over her lips twice, forcing them apart.

"Open your mouth. I'll just put the head inside."

She found this amusing and smiled; they all said that. And just like the others, Ernest took advantage of her parted lips and pushed his glans into her mouth. She put her tongue on it to stop him. They both froze. It was always very intense for her when a bloke put his thing in her mouth for the first time. But this bloke had manners. He didn't move. Reassured, she let her tongue explore his cock. She immediately recognised the taste that she'd had in her mouth earlier and was sure that he'd already popped it in while she was asleep. Instead of shocking her, it turned her on. She sucked the head like a big lollipop and let the whole cock penetrate her. She thought that he really must have fucked her mother with it and that explained the distinctive, slightly brackish taste. She closed her eyes so as to concentrate better and swirled her tongue around the glans very fast. She called this doing the propeller. Ernest yanked off the duvet. She felt cold air on her stomach and thighs. She opened her legs so that he could get a good view of her pussy. With his other hand, he extricated her breasts from her nightie.

"That's right, yes, show me your beauties. Spread your legs, show me your cunt."

With his cock knocking the back of her throat, he explored her pubic hair and her oozing slit.

She moved her head back, letting go of his cock.

"I'm a virgin, so be careful, OK?"

"You, a virgin?"

They both looked down at Ernest's fingers foraging around in her pink cleft. He pressed a little, felt the warm flesh yield

117

"As soon as it hurts, let me know and I'll pull out. And then, we'll try again until it's wider. All right?"

She nodded and arched her back to open her anus. He saw some pink flesh in the centre of the brown bull's eye. He put the head of his cock into her slit to get it nice and wet, then pressed it into the corolla of the anus and pushed with infinite gentleness. Bébé, who at first had been tense for she had not been accustomed to such gentleness with other partners, was pleasantly surprised by such consideration, and relaxed. The glans slipped into her anus like a large suppository.

"There, we'll stay like that as long as you want. OK? Just the head."

"OK."

Her voice was wavering, but it wasn't from apprehension. He started to tease her pussy at the front and, with his other hand, he grabbed hold of a breast to hold her tightly for when he'd ram it in right up to her heart, as if he were skewering her. The little cutie would get a right shock! He could feel her little heart pounding under his palm; she must have been scared for her heart to beat like that, but she also seemed to enjoy it.

But, just as he was about to run her through, he changed his mind. Why not savour her for a change? This girl was depraved, it would be more enjoyable to take it slowly rather than rip her apart like an old lag. He felt her strain, with her anus, to engulf his glans. He pushed as well and drove it in by an inch or so.

"Ouch! Gently! Gently!"

"Did I hurt you? Do you want me to pull out?"

"No, you can push it further in, but be gentle."

He pushed harder, gaining another inch.

"Make an 'O' with your mouth, as if you were surprised."

Intrigued, she obeyed. Her buttocks immediately relaxed and she felt her anus dilate. She moaned with surprise. Just like that, his cock had entered her fully like a big fish. It hadn't been painful. Ernest's bollocks dangled between her thighs; she could see them from underneath. It made her giggle and she reached down to stroke them.

"I can feel you inside me and I don't feel sore. I can feel you almost up to my stomach."

"It's nice, isn't it? D'you like it?"

"Yes. They're so big." She was cupping his balls. "Why are they so big?"

"Because they're full. But I'm going to empty them, OK? I'll bugger you hard now."

"Oh yes, bugger me, bugger me hard."

He heard her beginning to cry and was disconcerted. She had just remembered the boarding-school that was awaiting her and that it was the last time she was using her arse, at least in the next few months.

Ernest pulled out halfway and then rammed it back in. She was crying, but she was wide open. He could slide it in and out easily now, she felt as good in her arse as others did in their pussies.

"Fuck, I'm going to come," he grunted, losing his self-control. "I can't hold it in any longer, get ready for a big surprise!"

He almost pulled out, with only the tip of his penis still inside her, and was about to ram it deep inside her, just to make her yell her lungs out. In that moment of perfect silence, pregnant with expectation, they heard the floorboards creak downstairs.

"My mother! It's my mother!" whispered Bébé. "It's her I can recognise her step. She's trying not to make any noise

so as not to wake anyone." He listened. There was another stealthy creak. Someone was coming up the stairs with the utmost care.

"Oh God, she mustn't find you here, she mustn't!"

He frantically withdrew, picked up his bag and looked for an exit. There wasn't one. He was cornered. Bébé was sitting on the bed. She pointed to the window.

"Go onto the window ledge and I'll call you as soon as she's gone. She's just checking whether I'm asleep, I know what she's like. Maybe she felt sorry for me. Quickly. My brother's had to do this before; you'll be fine."

He looked for his trousers but couldn't find them. He must have kicked them under the bed; in any case, there wasn't time to look for them, the stealthy footsteps had reached the landing and in a few seconds, her mother would be in the room. He let himself be guided to the window which Bébé quietly opened. He leaned over. She showed him the ledge, which was quite wide, a sort of cornice which supported a gutter. Being a burglar, he could figure it out easily. He stepped over the window-frame, scraping his nuts in the process, and put both feet onto the ledge. He then moved sideways and hid behind the shutter while Bébé closed the window.

He hoped that she wouldn't take too long to get rid of her mother because, without his kecks, he was freezing his bollocks off out there. Not to mention that he could be seen, thanks to the star-lit sky. He'd look a right wally if a sleepless neighbour looked out of the window and saw him there, bollock-naked, clutching the ivy that covered the wall.

Not only was he freezing, but his balls were so swollen from the inflow of semen that they felt as if they were about to explode. There was such a build-up that he could feel

shooting pains in his prostate, as if someone were sticking red hot needles into it. He hoped that Bébé had had time to hide the trousers that he'd left on the floor at the foot of the bed. If her mother found them, he was done for. He could wave goodbye to social rehabilitation.

Chapter Eleven: A full-frontal spanking

After drawing the curtain, Bébé ran to her bed. She spotted Ernest's trousers and bundled them under her mattress. She hoped that she'd have enough time to jump into bed and pretend she was asleep. Her mother wouldn't dare wake her and would go back to bed, and she could bring Ernest back inside. She reached over to switch off the bedside lamp as she slid one leg under the duvet. Too late. Before she'd had time to switch off the light, the door opened and in came Bob in his black silk pyjamas. He was surprised to find her starkers.

"Why aren't you asleep? Why is your light on?" He closed the door behind him and put on the slippers that he was holding.

"Why have you got nothing on? Are you too hot? And why are you up?"

Bébé got under the duvet and pulled it up to her chin.

"I went for a pee, is that OK with you? And I can sleep naked if I want to. What's it to you? And now, piss off, I've seen enough of you, you bastard!"

"Don't be upset, sweetie," said Bob, stretching his arms in front of him in that imploring gesture that had worked so well on her mother. "I only came up to discuss the matter with you. You were a bit unfair earlier." Unfair! That was rich coming from him!

"What about you? You betrayed me!"

"I had no choice, Bébé. I had to protect myself. You were accusing me, I had to retaliate. Put yourself in my shoes!"

What a wanker! Such cynicism left her speechless. While

she was trying to find something to retort, he sat on the chair previously occupied by Ernest. She thought of the poor jailbird, standing on that ledge without a stitch on. She had to get rid of this two-faced bastard as quickly as possible.

"Get out of my room, Bob, d'you hear? Now! Or I'll call Mum. Then she'll see if it's me who keeps jumping on you as soon as her back's turned."

"You wouldn't do that," said Bob calmly. "You're not that stupid. Don't forget that I didn't tell your mother everything. I didn't tell her about your brother."

He saw that his answer had hit home.

"A cousin doesn't count," he continued, "but a brother... think of your mother's narrow-mindedness and her religious education. Incest..."

He let the word linger so as to leave its mark on her mind. She knew he was right; her mother, given time, would forgive her everything, but not that.

"You're really nasty, d'you know that?"

He pretended to look humble.

"I do my best, love. But I could point out that you don't have the highest morals either."

"What do you want from me? Spit it out!"

"Can't you guess?"

Looking very relaxed, Bob crossed his legs. It took a while for the penny to drop. It was just too outrageous, she couldn't believe it. After what had happened, he still had the front to...

"I hope you're joking. How can you even consider it for a moment? I'll tell you something. You make my flesh crawl. I'd rather die, so there!"

"We can't leave it there, my sweet," said Bob in a honeyed tone, "you should always finish what you've started."

Bébé shivered with anger. If looks could kill, her step-father would have been a goner. The swine had her where he wanted her and was revelling in her powerlessness. Her mother must never learn about Bertrand or she'd put him in boarding-school as well, she'd do her best to separate them forever. Her kid brother; he was a part of her, she couldn't do that to him. Anger gave way to despair and she burst into tears.

"Oh Bob, why are you so horrible? You wouldn't do that, would you? You wouldn't tell her about Bertrand? He hasn't done anything to you."

If she thought she could use tears to soften him up, she had another think coming. Bob settled himself even more comfortably in the chair.

"Of course I won't tell her... because you and I will come to an arrangement. You're not that stupid, are you? If you do it with others, you can do it with me as well. It makes sense."

Sitting on her bed with her legs bent, Bébé put her forehead on her knees and started to cry again. She had now completely forgotten about Ernest and was thinking about what was going to happen now. Because naturally, she knew she had to go through with it. She had no choice. She hugged her legs and, sobbing, buried her forehead between her knees. As she cried, she was prepared for the moment when her step-father would touch her. She knew that he would do it; she was naked, all he had to do was pull down the duvet and put his hand between her legs. As soon as anyone touched her pussy or put a finger in her arse, she was all theirs, and he knew it. But Bob let her have a good cry without trying it on. He waited for her to lift her somewhat surprised face and look at him quizzically through her tears.

"I don't want to force you to do anything," he murmured, "it has to come from you."

"What do you want?" she answered. She sniffed. He handed her a tissue and waited for her to blow her nose. Again, she questioned him with her eyes. She might as well get it over with, since she had to.

"Aren't you too warm under that duvet?"

So that was it. She shrugged and folded it back onto her feet. Sitting naked in the middle of the bed, with her knees raised and her tits squashed against her thighs, she really looked delightful, with tears running down her cheeks. Bob uncrossed his legs to give more room to John Thomas who was peeking out of his pyjama bottoms. When she saw his erect penis, Bébé batted her eyelids. She was getting turned on, it started in her guts and on her nipples. She had always loved being coerced, there was something of the submissive female in her. That's why she often let herself be 'raped' by her brother's mates, she liked to push them to their limits. Her breathing accelerated when she saw Bob move his chair forward. He pointed to the pillows and bolster.

"Pile them up in the centre of the bed, where you're sitting. Then come and sit on the edge of the mattress, facing me."

When she realised what he had in mind, she did as he said, then leaned back on the pile, facing Bob. Their knees were touching. Because he was waiting, she spread her legs so that he could ogle her pussy and propped herself up on her elbows.

"Lift up your legs and put your feet on the mattress. I want to see your arsehole as well."

She did as she was told and shamelessly displayed all her charms to him. He lowered his eyes and peered into her open

flesh and her dark little star. Bébé felt her nipples stiffen as well as a familiar tingling in her loins.

"You really are vile! I'm practically your daughter!"

"Don't be silly. Open your cunt, spread your legs wider." She did so. "You're soaking, you slut. Worse than your mother. I've never seen such a pair of women for getting so wet."

She found this reference to what he did with her mother strangely moving. Bob still hadn't touched her, he seemed content to simply admire her crotch. The tingling inside her became more pronounced, especially in her loins, and her clitoris was stiff.

"Do you remember what you told me earlier?"

She'd said a lot of things. Looking straight at him, she shook her head. Why did they all love looking at her pussy so much? It was only a slit with hairs around it!

"That I took advantage, when I was spanking you, and fingered you? Do you remember?"

She quickly nodded. He showed her his forefinger.

"Well, now I'm going to put my finger inside you for real. And I'll be facing you so that you can see it too."

He proceeded to do what he'd said. He ran his finger down from her clitoris. She felt as if she'd received an electric shock. His finger went back up, teased the clit, then back down again. Breathing unevenly, she looked at Bob, then at his finger. She was as red as a beetroot and quivering from head to foot. His finger was leaving no nook untouched, it alternately delved and hovered.

"So, are you still complaining? I'm touching your pussy now. I'm not just pretending. Can you feel it? Can you feel my finger?"

"Yes, Bob, I can feel it."

He made it run up and down several times and every time it went up, he'd lecherously tease her clit.

"I'll put it in your arse now, d'you mind? Answer me."

"No, Bob, I don't mind."

He pushed it deep inside her anus. Bébé gasped.

"You see, your holes belong to me now. I'll touch you whenever I feel like it and you'll let me. You're not so full of yourself now, are you? That'll teach you to be indignant."

He pushed his finger in and out; her anus clenched and relaxed spasmodically. With her mouth open and a stupid look on her face, Bébé let herself go.

"You like it, don't you? Don't tell me otherwise."

"You're right, Bob, I do like it. Oh God, what'll become of me in boarding-school?"

"Don't worry, the dykes will take care of you. They won't leave you to dry up."

He wanked her for a moment with both hands, teasing her cunt and foraging deep inside her rectum. She leaned back on both hands and lifted her pelvis; she was so open and panting. The juice was pouring out of her.

"Can you feel me touching your clit? And can you feel that thermometer in your arse?"

She nodded. She could feel everything. I'm a real slag, she thought, I have no shame. They can do anything they like to me, I'll do anything!"

"You'll have to open yourself up even more now."

She couldn't believe her ears. She tried to laugh, but it caught in her throat. How could she possibly be more open than she was now? He calmly explained it to her. He made her grab hold of her ankles and lie back on the bed, against the pile of pillows, lifting her legs up in the air while doing the splits. She

practically choked in that position.

"Oh Bob, you're really disgusting, making me get into this position. What are you going to do?"

"I'm going to give you the spanking you deserve, you shameless little tart! A frontal spanking!"

"Frontal? Oh Bob, do you mean?"

"On your pussy, exactly, sweetie."

"Oh Bob, you really have some strange ideas. You're twisted, you know? On the... You won't hit me too hard, will you? It must hurt a lot there."

"I'll hit you just hard enough. You'll see, you'll love it. Your mother goes crazy when I do it to her."

Bébé quivered. She found it difficult to imagine her mother in that position. He knelt in front of her and, very gently at first, tapped on her pussy with the flat of his hand. A feeling of heat rushed up into her belly. This thing was amazing, creating incredible sensations. Each slap would make her cleft wider, her compressed labia would flatten and a mini electric shock would course through her clitoris. It radiated as far as her breasts and her throat.

"Oh Bob, Bob..."

He accelerated the rhythm and hit her harder; in this position, her pussy was very dilated, and the slaps directly hit her flesh, making her juices spatter.

"Oh, naughty Bob," cooed Bébé in admiration, "you're such a pervert."

"Me? I bet you like it though!"

"Oh, I do, I do! But it's still a depraved thing to do! Hit me harder, I feel hot all over. It hurts but it's so nice. You know how to touch me... No-one else has ever done this to me before. Oh please, lick me a bit, I'm so turned on, it's burning me..."

"I can do better than that," said Bob, standing up again.

He put his cock in her slit. Bébé's eyes goggled and she breathed haltingly. She was so open in this incredible position and so aroused by the spanking on her pussy that he had no difficulty whatsoever in inserting his glans into her vagina.

"Bob, you bastard!" she cried. "Don't do that!"

He looked at her and smiled, with his glans in her hole. Another half an inch and it would all be over.

"You're not going to keep your cherry all your life, are you?"

"No, Bob, don't do it! Not there! Put it in my arse if you like, but not there! Please, I'm being a good girl, I'm letting you do everything you want with me. But not that..."

He hesitated. He couldn't understand why this little sexpot was denying herself the best bit.

"If you do it, I'll tell Mum," she threatened. "I swear I'll tell her."

She felt the big head slide in and out of her; she didn't dare move in case she made a false move and inadvertently gave in to the penetration. She had promised her brother that he could take her virginity on the eve of her wedding day. She didn't want to spoil that. She was drenched in a cold sweat. She was all the more terrified because she didn't trust herself; if Bob pushed it in, she knew in advance that she would be delighted, she so wanted to feel a prick in that orifice. But she couldn't do that to her brother. She'd promised him! She pouted and started to snivel.

"Are you crying, Bébé? Darling, are you crying? Are you cross with Mummy? Are you crying all alone in your little bed?"

They both froze in panic, stuck together like a couple of dogs in the street. Terrified, they looked at each other. Laura

was slurring her speech from the sleeping pills and stumbled over each syllable, like a drunk.

"Mummy will comfort you... Don't cry, you naughty girl. It's for your own good that I'm sending you to boarding-school. We'll soon find you a husband..."

Without thinking, she turned the doorknob. Frozen in horror, Bob silently leapt towards the door and pushed against it with all his might. Meanwhile, a wide-eyed Bébé was straightening her bed at top speed; she put the pillows and the bolster at the head of the bed and dived under the duvet which she pulled up to her chin. Her mother and her step-father were both pushing on either side of the door.

"Damn," muttered Laura, "you silly cow, you've left the key downstairs." She leaned over to speak through the keyhole and raised her voice. "I'm just going to get the key, you wait here. I didn't mean to wake you, poppet. I was looking for Bob. He's not in bed, I wonder where he's got to at this time of night."

They heard her shuffling downstairs. Bob was confused. Why was she going to get the key if the door wasn't locked? Hang on, why wasn't it locked? He clearly remembered Laura locking it earlier. There was something fishy going on, but he'd have to figure it out later. Right now, there were more pressing matters to attend to. He carefully half-opened the door. His wife was halfway down the stairs. He tiptoed onto the landing, silently closed the door, and hugging the walls, went upstairs. He could hide there until Laura returned to her daughter's room, then he would regain the marital bed. He was halfway up the stairs when he heard Laura stop.

"Bob can't be in her room," she muttered (she always prattled away to herself like a sleepwalker when she'd popped her

bloody pills). "He can't be in there because the door's locked. I'll let her sleep; I'll go upstairs and look in on Bertrand, maybe Bob's in his room."

"And why in God's name would I be in that prat's room?" thought Bob indignantly. "Does she take me for a poofter or what?" When she was drugged up like that and woke up practically comatose, Laura couldn't think straight. He watched her come back up. She was tottering. Those pills were knocking her out again. She was fighting sleep and went up the stairs as if in a dream. Maybe she was dreaming? She certainly wasn't wide awake. He knew from experience that by morning, she'd remember nothing. He'd often find her asleep in another room and have to bring her back to bed.

Having returned to the first-floor landing, Laura was losing her battle against sleep. She felt incredibly heavy all of a sudden and dropped onto her knees. With a sigh that was almost one of pleasure, she lay down on the landing in front of Bébé's door and started snoring.

"Now what am I going to do?" thought Bob. What should he do? Go back downstairs, stepping over her? What if she woke up? She'd understand everything. She often had glimmers of lucidity during these sleepwalking fits. He didn't want to risk it. It was more sensible to wait in Ernest's room for her to come round. He felt better after making that decision. He turned on his heels and opened the guest bedroom door. Ernest would understand, he was a man of the world. Bob froze on the threshold; the light was on, but the bed was empty and the window was open.

"Where'd that bastard go?"

He put two and two together: the door that had been locked, then unlocked; Ernest's toolbag. It all made sense!

The swine! He leaned out of the window and what did he see but Ernest standing on the gutter, half-naked, legging it over Bébé's window frame! Judas! Toerag! What a shit! He'd show him! But suddenly, he looked again. Ernest still had one leg dangling out of the window. Bob slapped his thighs gleefully.

Ernest wasn't entering Bébé's room, but her brother's room. That was the best one yet! Ernest had turned into a poof! He'd seen it all now. He must have picked up bad habits in the nick; having fucked so many queers, he must have acquired a taste for it. Beaming, Bob climbed into Ernest's bed. He certainly wasn't sleepy, but he'd be more comfortable there to witness the events that were to follow.

CHAPTER TWELVE: THE KID BROTHER

E rnest had been perching semi-naked on the gutter for a good ten minutes and he was not amused. Why didn't Bébé let him back in? His fingers ached from hanging on to the ivy, not to mention that he was getting very cold. A bitter wind had got up and was whipping his nuts. He had no intention of hanging around until dawn. He looked up and tried to figure out what to do next. His bedroom window, which he had left open, was just above Bébé's window. If he clung to the ivy and scaled the wall by using the shutter latches and the drainpipe as footholds, it couldn't be that difficult for a skilled cat-burglar like himself to clamber back into his room. However, seven years had passed since he had last scaled a wall, and he felt a little rusty. He had put on weight in jail and wasn't as supple as he used to be. He'd feel a right idiot if he fell off and had to be carted off to hospital with a broken leg, or worse, and all that for a bit of crumpet. He had to think of something. He had always been susceptible to chest infections; already, the cold was spreading up from his bollocks into his belly. If she left him out there any longer, he would surely catch his death.

While he was brooding over all this, he was constantly searching for an exit. That's how he noticed, without really looking, that the next window along was ajar. He knew it was the kid brother's room. What if he went back in that way? The little angel was probably fast asleep and wouldn't hear a thing. All he had to do was cross his room and make it back upstairs to fetch another pair of kecks before getting back to business. He

started to move along sideways, hugging the wall like a lizard, and felt his cock scrape against the render. Looking down, he saw to his disbelief that he still had a hard-on. It was as stiff as a poker. Lord, he must have caused himself some internal damage by stopping short just before shooting his load. In theory, the cold makes your goolies shrivel up, but not this time. He'd never had such a boner. He sucked in his stomach so as to avoid grazing it again and reached the brother's window. Cursing under his breath, he slid his hand inside, lifted the latch, pushed open one of the panes, stepped over the sill and found himself in the warm room. It was only once he was inside that he started shivering all over, which was probably a delayed reaction. With his teeth chattering, he fumbled his way to the door. It was pitch dark in there. Halfway across the room, he bumped into a small table that he hadn't seen and something came crashing down onto the floor.

"Bloody typical," he thought. The light immediately came on, blinding him before he could make out the brother in his lilac silk pyjamas sitting bolt upright in bed, his face as white as a sheet.

"Oh, it's you," he said, "you gave me a fright. I thought you were a burglar." Feeling rather foolish, he then remembered that Bob's cousin was precisely that, and that he'd just done time for burglary. He then spotted the toolbag that Ernest was carrying, the stethoscope around his neck and finally his bollocks dangling between his hairy legs. Ernest petulantly lifted up his shirt to show him his dick. It was still rock hard.

"What are you staring at? Have you never seen one before?"

"What do you want from me?" whispered Bertrand, blushing like a virgin. He could not bring himself to look away from the imposing red boner sticking out of the tuft of frizzy hair.

"What do I want?"

He made up his mind instantly. Since the little poppet was awake, he may as well make himself useful. If his sister hadn't opened the window for him, it was because something had come up. Perhaps her mother had got into bed with her to comfort her. But the brother was available and Ernest wanted to do something about his swollen balls. It wasn't healthy to stay like that, he had to drain them. He looked at the teenager more closely. Sixteen years old, but as fresh as a daisy. And as cute as a button.

"I want you to give me a blow-job, sweetie, that's what I want. Then I'll go back to bed, with a light heart and empty balls. What can I say? I got used to getting my end away every night in the nick. There's no shortage of poofs inside, I can tell you, all you have to do is take your pick. Come on, suck me off, it's top drawer stuff!"

He threw his bag onto the bed, which made the poor kid jump, and marched towards him. His fat prick swung menacingly with each step.

"If you take one more step, I'll scream for help," threatened the sprog in a strangled voice reminiscent of an old dear getting her bag nicked.

"I'd love to hear you scream for help. Do you want me to tell your dear mother what you get up to with your sister, you dirty little bastard? You should be ashamed of yourself. A sister is sacred, you must be really deviant..."

Twenty minutes earlier, that devil's advocate had championed the opposing view, but this did not bother him in the slightest. What mattered to him right now was emptying his goolies.

"How..? How do you..? Who told you..?" The poor cherub was stammering from the shock. Having reached the bed,

Ernest tore off the duvet. Lilac silk pyjamas! It's all right for some! Others have to do a seven-year stretch cooped up in a cell measuring twelve feet by twelve with three other guys, and the stench of the latrines.

"She told me. I've just fucked her. I also fucked your mother. There's no reason why I shouldn't fuck you as well. It's free of charge!"

This guy was crazy! Panic-stricken, Bertrand cowered in his bed.

"Don't hurt me!" he begged.

"I won't hurt you any more than you hurt your sister, laddie. Take that off. You can keep your shirt on, I don't want you catching the sniffles."

Bertrand understood what was in store for him and began to feel feverish. He'd done a few things with Jéréme, but never with a grown-up. And never all the way. Mostly hand relief when Bébé wasn't available.

Ernest peeled off his pyjama bottoms in seconds and put a hand between the boy's thighs. He liked to toss off these little sissies while he was buggering them. Theirs were not proper cocks yet, but more like oversized clitorises that ran to seed. He gently rubbed Bertrand's barely pubescent balls and his slim velvety penis. The sly little devil spread his legs.

"Have you ever given a blow-job before?"

"Are you crazy? No, never," lied Bébé's brother. He couldn't take his eyes off the red-hot poker that was swinging in front of his eyes. Bloody hell, it was massive, he'd never be able to take it! A delicious shudder of fear ran up his spine and he felt his penis twitch. Ernest was laughing.

"Are you getting hard, laddie? Are you getting into it now?"

"Please, don't do that to me! I'd hate myself afterwards."

"You say that, but it grows on you. The first time I was buggered against my will in jail, there were four guys holding me down. I would have killed them if I could. But you see, I got over it. And I even enjoy getting it up the arse now. It's different."

He exposed the whippersnapper's sensitive glans and leaned over to examine it more closely.

"Spread your legs, sweetie, show me your family jewels."

A flushed Bertrand lifted his pyjama shirt and did as he was told. The con's callous fingers touched him with alarming gentleness and revealed his timid maleness like a pink candle on a birthday cake, with the glans looking like a maraschino cherry. Ernest delicately began to wank him off. He sat on the bed and pushed Bertrand back, forcing him to lie down. Bertrand closed his eyes with shame. The con's other hand caressed his thighs. He was even more gentle than Bébé. He felt goose pimples covering his entire body and bent a leg. Ernest chuckled when he saw the dark circle of his anus. They no longer had to spell things out to each other. It's always the same story with those shy young boys, all you have to do is tickle their winkle and then they're all yours, they yield like wicker that's been soaked overnight. (In jail, Ernest had done a course in basket-weaving; well, you have to keep busy...).

"D'you know where I've been, laddie?"

"Er... my sister's room?"

Ernest had a good chuckle. Then, as he was bringing off Bertrand, he sucked his forefinger and felt the boy's anus. It clenched and Ernest tutted so a frightened Bertrand relaxed his buttocks. He inserted his fingertip into the boy's anus.

"No, stupid, I've been to a strange world. D'you know where that is? It's the nick. Everything's topsy-turvy there. I thought

that if I came back here, everything would be normal again. But it's even worse! This place is crazier than the nick. A sister who's sleeping with her brother, a pharmacist who collects Russian bonds and pops pills as if they were sweets! I'm going to end up thinking that the whole world has gone mad... open up your arse, darling, so that I can get my finger in easily."

He squeezed the cherub's stiff little prick in his rough hand and pushed his finger right up into his arse. He expected the kid to protest vehemently, but he didn't. He also expected his anus to open up, and indeed it did. He was able to slide his finger in and out without any hindrance. There's nothing like a little massage of their prostate to whet their appetite.

"You'd be really cute, you know, in a mini-skirt, wearing some black eye-shadow and lipstick. You'd look like a real young lady. In the nick, we'd often dress up our pansies, there would be Miss Prison competitions. We'd make them wear black stockings and high heels. We'd have a ball."

The poor sprog was taking all this in without batting an eyelid. Ernest stopped beating him off and pulled his finger out of his arse. He sniffed it. There was no smell at all. Definitely a good point. Ernest wasn't too keen on shit. He leaned over, grabbed Bertrand by the neck and forced him to sit up on the edge of the bed with his legs dangling, and then pushed his cock into the boy's face. Bertrand recoiled, but a slap made him see sense and he immediately opened his mouth while putting a hand to his cheek. He was the type to enjoy a beating. Ernest grabbed him by the ears, as if he were holding a vase by its handles, and rammed his cock deep into his throat. He felt the youngster's tongue going all over the place and a jolt from his gag reflex. He backed away; he didn't want him to choke.

He pulled out his tool and showed him the glans glistening with saliva.

"I was just testing you, darling. I don't really fancy a blow-job, what I want is something a bit tighter than a mouth. Come on, turn over. I'm sure I don't need to spell it out to you."

Bertrand felt almost disgusted, but at the same time, he was brimming with a horrible curiosity. He adopted the position that he had made his sister take so many times. When Ernest saw him arch his back to spread his buttocks, he shook his head in disbelief. The dark star of his anus opened up above a pair of very cute and downy balls which looked like two fledglings. He placed his saliva-coated penis in the centre of the bistre-coloured circle and, clutching it in one hand, he pulled Bertrand towards him by placing his hand under his belly. The boy gasped with surprise when it entered him.

"Ow! Gently, Mister Ernest, gently!"

"It's only the tip and you're already whingeing? You're a real wimp, aren't you? Wait till our four nuts meet, two in front, two behind, then you'll really notice the difference when I've pushed it all in."

He forced it in a few more inches. The kid was tight, but not too much, it was just right. Bertrand groaned again, but this time with horrified surprise.

"You like it, don't you? Does it surprise you? Wait, my love, it's not all in yet. So, do you like my trouser-snake?"

He stroked the pansy's damp belly and clasped his willy. It was so stiff it made him laugh.

"You're as hard as a grown-up! I'll end up thinking you quite enjoy taking it up the arse!" Indeed, Bertrand's sphincter was relaxing; the dear boy clearly enjoyed it. Soon their balls were touching.

"Can you feel them? You've got four of them now. Two little ones and two big ones. Wait till I empty the big ones, I bet you'll like that."

He who takes it slow and steady goes a long way. Ernest was in no hurry. His rhythm was regular. The internal resistance had disappeared, it was sliding in and out beautifully. The little cutie was as soft and warm as a girl inside. It made a nice change from jail queers with whom he'd sometimes had the feeling of fucking an old sock. This boy was as fresh as a daisy with a delightfully pert and plump bottom and baby-soft skin. Not to mention that he was a real little perv with a greedy arse, even worse than his sister!

"You've learned a few things today, haven't you? You know how to fix a washbasin, change a distributor and play a three card trick. And now, you've learnt how to offer your arse to an old lag like me! Your mates will be well impressed tomorrow when you tell them."

A shiver ran down Bertrand's spine. The disgust that he'd ignored earlier came flooding back at the sound of Ernest's coarse cackle. A poof! He was a poof! Furious with himself, he began to sob hoarsely and bitterly. The convict's prick was banging away at him rhythmically. Bertrand felt that it was almost a part of him now, that he'd always feel it inside him, even once it was over. It hadn't just penetrated his arse, but his entire soul, where it would leave an indelible stain. Like Bob earlier, whose experience of being flogged with his own belt had awakened unknown sensations within him, Bertrand thought of his sister and wondered, "Is that what it feels like to her?" Experiencing so much pleasure disgusted him and made him cry even more.

"You're crying, but your arse is nice and open," said Ernest

mockingly, "and your winkle's as hard as a poker. Don't cry. You'll see, you'll grow to enjoy it. I bet you that in six months' time, you'll be cottaging, you'll be offering your services to old men."

That was exactly what Bertrand was afraid of. He remembered the way he and his friends used to make fun of the queers they'd see in town. And now he was one of them!

"Oh please, Mister Ernest, please, can you finish off now? Do what you have to do and... and..."

"You must be joking! This is the best bit. You'll see, we'll both come at the same time. You'll come all over the sheets and I'll come in your arse."

"No, don't touch me! I don't want to!"

But he didn't push away Ernest's hand, which was around his penis again. The bastard gently teased his glans and foreskin.

"Let's play a little game, OK? I'll bugger you and I'll wank your clit at the same time. Can you feel me shoving it into your arse and peeling your clit? Now I'm pulling out and pulling up your foreskin. And again. Don't tell me you don't like it, because I wouldn't believe you. I'm ramming it into your arse and wanking your clit. Whack, whack, whack. Oh God, I can feel it coming..."

"Me too," confessed Bertrand huskily. The despicable and terrifying pleasure that he was experiencing was unlike anything he'd ever felt, even with his sister.

"Me too," he repeated, "oh, it's coming, Mister Ernest, it's coming!"

There was a tremor in his voice. Ernest's hand slowed down but his thrusts accelerated. And suddenly, it happened; they moaned in unison, blending their voices, Bertrand's falsetto and Ernest's baritone, like cantors striking up a hymn to pleasure.

Then they collapsed on top of each other, one inside the other, letting the spunk gush out spasmodically like blood spurting from a severed artery. Bertrand bucked as he felt Ernest's semen flooding his bowels, as well as his own spraying all over the sheets. Then it calmed down and they remained still.

After a while, Ernest withdrew. Bertrand was so filled with shame that he didn't dare turn around but preferred to bury his face in the pillow. Ernest stroked his bottom.

"That was nice. Was it good for you?"

"Yes, it was good for me," he had to admit miserably.

He shivered. He felt the convict cover him with the duvet, a gesture which strangely moved him. He had the feeling that he was a wife with her husband. He was running the gamut of contradictory emotions; he would feel depressed to the point of considering suicide one minute and then on the verge of hysterical laughter the next.

"You know what?" whispered the convict into his hair. "I'm going to sleep with you. I'm feeling too lazy to go back upstairs."

Bertrand felt his hairs stand on end on his arms and legs.

"But... you can't be serious... we'll be on top of each other, it's a single bed."

"We'll just have to sleep one inside the other," replied Ernest. "Give me your little arse, I'll show you. Give it here."

"Again?"

"Yes, again, But don't be scared, I'll just pop it inside, that way we can sleep joined together, like newlyweds. Come on give it to me."

Bertrand sighed meekly and, bending one knee, spread his thighs while Ernest stuck it back in effortlessly.

"Looks like you're a fast learner. You're like a good little wife. Did you notice how easily it went in?"

"Yes..."

When it was all in, Bertrand straightened his leg and Ernest tenderly put his arms around him, clasping him to his stomach.

"I won't be able to sleep like this," grumbled Bertrand, "I can feel it, it's too big."

"I can feel you as well; but that won't stop me getting some shut-eye. You'll soon get used to it. I like to keep it warm when I'm asleep, it gives me sweet dreams. And if you feel it getting hard during the night, don't worry. I might even shoot another load inside you, it'll grease your bowels, that way you won't need any laxatives."

Bertrand couldn't help chuckling oddly. It was so weird to fall asleep with a cock in his bum. As the convict's prick filled out in the warmth of his rectum, Bertrand could feel his own penis twitching out of sympathy. He stroked it.

"Are you playing with yourself, you dirty boy? Let daddy do it."

Bertrand deliciously let him take over. Ernest's callous hand closed around it as if it were a captive bird.

"In jail, I'd often sleep like this with my little pansy. I'd always fuck him in the morning before I went for a piss. Admit that you don't dislike it."

"No, I don't, and I even... I even like it!"

They laughed, in the same suppressed and coarse way. Ernest suddenly thought, "Isn't life great?" Everything was going really well for him, in fact it was going like a dream. He'd found himself a little slag, a queer, they were going to get him a job, he knew where to nick some dosh if he needed any. He could take it easy.

"Bob? Are you in there, Bob? Are you in Bertrand's room? Are you hiding just to wind me up?"

They both sat bolt upright, then, with some difficulty, managed to disentangle themselves, like two snails that have got stuck together and that have to be prised apart like sucker pads. That pain-in-the-neck was back again, and she was still out of it.

"Oh please, Mister Ernest, she mustn't find you here."

Ernest totally agreed. He grabbed his Dr Kildare bag, the stethoscope and charged towards the window. For crying out loud, this in-and-out-of-windows business was getting tedious! It was like a bad farce. The little squirt closed the window behind him. Ernest was still drowsy from the warmth of the bed. He looked down at the grass beneath him. He was only on the first floor, he could always jump. But he didn't have any trousers on. What would he do bollock-naked? He looked up on the off chance. Well lit by a streetlamp, his cousin was watching him mockingly from the upstairs window.

"Well, you don't look too clever down there," he scoffed. "Come on, you silly sod, I'll give you a hand up."

Ernest didn't hang about. He handed him his toolbag, which Bob flung into the room, then he stretched out his arm; carefully using the window sill as a foothold, Ernest managed to hoist himself up.

CHAPTER THIRTEEN: A MOMENT OF WEAKNESS

"What the hell are you doing in my room?" asked Ernest as he finally stepped over the window ledge.

"You can talk! What were you doing on the gutter?"

"I was hiding, believe it or not. Your missus almost caught me."

"Same here," laughed Bob. "I was downstairs in her daughter's room when Laura woke up. I made a hasty getaway because Laura is horribly jealous. Especially of her own daughter!"

"You bastard! So it was you..."

"What are you saying? What do you mean, it was me?"

Ernest beamed. That was the best one yet.

"I was with that little cock-sucker as well! When you tiptoed along, she thought it was her mum."

"Oh, the slut! Naturally, she didn't tell me that," seethed Bob. "Christ, so that's why she was so wet!"

"Did you think it was merely because of your charm? Well no, I was giving her a good seeing to when you arrived. It's incredible how much that little girl loves cock."

Bob laughed, but on the other side of his face. He was gutted. That Ernest was a crafty bugger! He was always quicker off the mark, and prison hadn't slowed him down. As soon as there was a piece of pussy in the vicinity, he had to go and dip his wick. So he'd managed to fuck the little slut. Why hadn't Bob buggered the little nympho straight away? He always had to beat about the bush.

"Did you come? Was it good?"

Ernest pulled a face.

"This is it, I didn't! I was on the brink, and then you came along. I had to go outside, and honestly, you should have seen my poor bollocks, they were like watermelons!"

Bob felt better on hearing this.

"So, let me get this right, you made up for it with the brother?" Bob wasn't into boys, but he was open-minded about these things.

"I had to empty the damn things," sighed Ernest, "or they would have burst."

They laughed their heads off. They hadn't really changed; they were the same rascals as in the old days. Neither jail nor marriage had changed them for the worse. There they were, doubled up with laughter on the bed, when they heard a timid knock on the door.

"Mister Ernest?" cooed Laura sleepily. "Is Bob with you? He's not in my bed."

It was that pain-in-the-neck again! Great. She wouldn't leave them alone that night.

"Mister Ernest? Are you asleep? I need to speak to you, I can't find Bob. Is he not in your room?"

"And why would he be in my room?" grunted Ernest. "What do you take us for? A couple of poofs, or what? We're cousins, not husband and wife!"

"Of course not! I never meant to offend you... I just thought..." And she started to snivel against the door. "He must have left. He's so proud and I must have offended him... I should never have hit him with the belt. It's my fault!"

"Hit him with a belt?"

A shamefaced Bob looked at his feet. Delighted, Ernest pointed to the bed.

"Hide under there," he whispered to his cousin. "I'll let her in for a moment, just long enough for her to calm down, then we'll both finish the night in the daughter's room."

Unthinkingly, though with some reluctance, Bob got on all fours and crawled under the bed. Ernest folded back the covers right down to the floor and sat on the mattress, with his cock still exposed.

"Come in, don't stay out there, you're in your own home, for Christ's sake!"

"I didn't want to disturb you," said Laura as she came in.

With tearful eyes and looking spaced-out from the sleeping pills, she didn't immediately notice that Ernest was half-naked. But he had sharp eyes and his wits about him. He could see that his cousin's wife was very dopey and she hadn't even had the presence of mind to put on a dressing-gown over her transparent nightie. She had entered the room of a bachelor who hadn't touched a woman for seven years and all she was wearing was this flimsy garment that concealed absolutely nothing and skimmed her buttocks; he realised that the night was far from over. He chuckled spitefully at the thought of Bob eating balls of fluff under the bed.

Wild-eyed, Laura staggered towards him.

"You've got to help me, Mister Ernest, you're his cousin. You have to explain to him that I don't really want a divorce, I only said that because I was pissed off with him. Oh God! When I think of that beating I gave him! He must really hate me, I know he must. He must be a long way away by now."

She sniffed and smiled sheepishly at her guest. Then her eyes widened and she put a hand over her mouth.

"Mister Ernest! Oh... you... your fly's undone," she whispered bashfully, pointing to the convict's crotch.

"Come again?" His gaze followed her finger. Good God! He was hard again. And how could he not be? She'd waltzed into his room wearing next to nothing, with her pussy on show beneath that piece of gauze, and on top of all that, she wanted to teach him a few manners!

"I'm sorry, cousin, I don't tend to sleep with my trousers on." He demurely covered up with a shirt-tail. "Is that better? Come and sit next to me and tell me all your worries. I can give you good advice when it comes to matters of the heart."

Having become aware of her immodest attire, Laura tried to back out of the room.

"God, I'm almost naked... I'd forgotten we had a guest in the house. Those blasted sleeping pills... I'll go and get my dressing-gown. I can't stay like this in your presence."

"Don't worry about me," said Ernest, feeling offended, "you're fine as you are, honest. The cut's a bit racy, I'll grant you that, but with your figure, you can wear whatever you like. Honestly, it really suits you. What's it made of? Is it silk?"

He touched her nightie and pulled her towards the bed. She feebly resisted and avoided looking at the cock that was protruding from his shirt-tails. It was impossible to ignore his hard-on. It was her own fault, she had to admit it, she should never have entered his room in the middle of the night with practically nothing on. She tried to fold her arm over her breasts and clenched her thighs to hide her bush.

"Please let go of me," she begged. "I really must go and get my dressing-gown. I didn't realise I was so indecent."

Let go of her? Not on your nellie! Not only did he not let go of her but he took her other hand.

"Come now, don't hide your beauties, give me your pretty little hands." He forced her to open out her arms and leered at everything that she was unintentionally displaying under that gossamer with such greed that Laura felt herself blush to the roots of her hair. She was sufficiently woozy to fail to react but she was nevertheless aware of what was happening.

"Mister Ernest, please..."

"You didn't answer me earlier. Is it silk?"

He took both her hands in one of his and with the other, he delicately touched the hem of her cobweb mini skirt, and pretended to examine its texture, lifting the baby doll to reveal her hairy crotch. Laura shivered. Why, oh why, did she not push him away? If Bob ever found out...

"No," she said with a tremor in her voice, "it's sheer nylon mesh, that's why it's so see-through."

She could see that the bastard was lifting the thing so as to ogle her pussy. Why did she let him? Those pills sometimes put her in a strange frame of mind; there were times when she would be dreaming yet convinced that it was real, and other times when the opposite would happen, it really was real, but the following morning, she'd wake up convinced she'd dreamt it.

"It's very pretty nylon, it really looks like silk."

Now he lifted the skirt above her navel. But she couldn't stop him because he was holding both her hands.

"It was a gift from Bob," she murmured. "In theory, I wear it for his eyes only, when the children are asleep. He likes sexy underwear."

"I don't blame him."

"He says that it gives him ideas..."

Well, he wasn't the only one. Although she was clenching her thighs, he was still shamelessly getting an eyeful.

"Oh God," mumbled Laura, "this must be a dream. I wouldn't let him get away with this otherwise."

Flabbergasted, Ernest's eyes widened. He couldn't believe how naïve, or hypocritical, she was.

"Of course it's all a dream, cousin," he murmured, "a dream we're both having..."

He made himself comfortable and opened his thighs to free John Thomas from beneath his shirt. He immediately noticed the 'dreamer's' misty gaze drift down towards it. She fluttered her eyelashes and her mouth formed a perfect 'O' but no sound came out of it.

"And from the back?" asked Ernest before she had time to regain her senses, "Does it look as pretty seen from the back?"

He made her twirl around and lifted her baby-doll to look at her arse. A wave of fire coursed up her belly. She gasped in horror. Over there, in the mirror, she could see herself from head to toe. God! Her hand went up to her face. It had to be a dream, thankfully she would have forgotten all about it tomorrow. Through the hazy fabric, she could see her breasts and her pubic hair, it was worse than if she'd been naked. Her 'naughty lingerie' drew attention to what it was supposed to conceal and that was precisely why Bob had bought this scandalous garment in an erotic supplies emporium (that's what she liked to call sex shops).

"You're taking advantage of me," said Laura (even in her dreams, she liked to protest). "You're very naughty... Oh God, I can see you, you know, in the mirror. You're pretending to

look at my nightie, but you're lifting it to look at my bottom. Oh, you are bad!"

"So what? Why shouldn't I admire it? It's a beautiful behind. I like gorgeous arses." The word made her shudder.

"Don't you find it big? Bob often makes me feel ashamed of it, he tells me it's too big."

"He doesn't have a clue. It's plump, but it's not big."

He cupped a buttock. Meanwhile, Bob was inhaling dust under the bed. He could see everything in the wardrobe mirror. He was shocked by his wife's passive behaviour.

"Oh, you're touching my bottom, Ernest, I can feel it, you know, don't think I don't realise what you're up to."

Frowning, she turned around and gazed at him with a look that was almost lucid, as if she had snapped back to reality.

"I was so distraught when I noticed that Bob was gone that I didn't think of putting on my dressing-gown. But I realise that I look indecent like this."

"I can see your tits and your muff through this," said Ernest.

Laura modestly tugged on her nightie, which squashed her breasts and made her nipples dilate like a pair of wide-open eyes.

"I know," she murmured, "it's my own fault. You're a man, and you just can't help yourself..."

Ernest's cock stood to attention in all its glory and his balls were spread out for all to see. He tried to cover himself again with his shirt and she was grateful to him for that. If things went too fast, she knew that her dream would come to an end and she would wake up feeling headachy, trying to hold on to shreds of the fantasy. And Bob would be lying next to her, snoring away.

"Come and sit on my lap," suggested Ernest, patting his

hairy thighs as if this was the most natural thing in the world. Laura tittered.

"Do you think I should?" It must be a dream; he would never have suggested such a thing in reality. He was Bob's cousin after all, some things only happen in dreams...

She let him pull her towards him and, tugging on her baby doll nightdress, she tried to sit diagonally across his lap. But at the last minute, he saw her turn around and back onto him so that she was straddling him and facing the mirror. The first thing she saw was her gaping pink slit in the dark fleece. She tried to bring her thighs together but he managed to slide a shin between her ankles to prevent her.

"But... but, Mister Ernest, I can't stay like this, look in the mirror, you can see everything..."

"I can't see anything at all," said Ernest dishonestly, "you've turned your back on me." But he was leering at her as much as he could over her shoulder.

"I'm so hairy," she mused, opening her legs slightly. And why shouldn't she, since he'd told her he couldn't see anything? It's funny how dreams work, you end up believing anything you're told. They both stared at her large hairy pussy spread out before them in the mirror.

"So hairy..." repeated Laura, crimson-faced. "Oh! I can see you, you know, I can see you in the mirror! You're looking at my privates!"

As quick as a flash, before she had time to bring her legs together again, he covered her moist slit with his palm.

"There you go," he whispered, "now I can't see it any more." Stunned, she didn't know what to say. His rough fingers folded over her pussy and one of them slid between her labia, pressing deliciously on her clitoris. What should she do? She decided to

remain in denial, because that seemed a lot less hassle.

"You're right. But don't take your hand away, otherwise you'll see everything again!"

She nestled against him and spread her legs wide. She'd never had such a dirty dream featuring a man other than her husband. Usually, when she had an erotic dream, it was always with Bob.

"I really must stop taking as much bloody Rohypnol," she told herself. "Bob's right, they'll make me unhinged in the end."

In the meantime, she was yielding to Ernest's insidious fingering; his fingers were inside her slit, so that her pussy was visible again in the mirror, but she decided that she couldn't see it. It was in this position that she told Ernest all her woes, while he fondled her and she pretended that she could see and feel nothing.

When she had finished, Ernest grabbed one of her tits. She slapped his fingers.

"What are you like? I'm telling you about Bob and you take advantage..." She stopped, with her mouth open. He had just squeezed her clitoris.

"I'll bring him back tomorrow, I promise," said Ernest, increasingly huskily, "I know where he is."

"You do? Really? Seriously?"

"I swear," answered Ernest. "First thing tomorrow, I'll bring him back, and he'll be all apologetic."

Disgusted by such cunning, Bob, who was powerlessly hiding under the bed, could see his cousin wanking Laura thanks to the mirror. He grabbed a handful of hairs on Ernest's leg and gave a good tug.

"Ow!" yelled Ernest, jumping up and turfing Laura off his lap.

"What happened?" Taken aback, she watched him rub his calf. The bloody bastard had ripped out a whole patch! Well, if that's how it was, he was going to get nasty, he'd shag his nympho of a pharmacist right in front of him!

"Come over here, we'll be more comfortable on a chair. There must be fleas in the bed."

"Nonsense! There aren't any fleas in my house!"

But Ernest wasn't listening. He grabbed a chair that was near the door and placed it in front of the wardrobe, about three feet away from it. He then sat down again, stretched out his legs in front of him and pulled Laura over to make her straddle him.

"Mister Ernest, you really are impossible! I can't sit on you so close to the mirror!"

"Do you want me to bring Bob back or not?"

"Of course I do, but..."

"Then you've got to be nice to me. I promise that he'll never find out about this. Go on, be a dear, look at the boner you've given me. It's all your doing. You have to make amends. You show me your pussy and your arse, have some mercy!"

She felt embarrassed because he was right. She let him get her to straddle him as before, except that it was a lot worse now. She could no longer be in denial. In the wardrobe mirror, she clearly saw that he was getting an eyeful. She tried to pull down her nightie because her slit, which was gaping like a starving mouth in her frizzy bush, was just too obscene. But he dissuaded her by slapping her hands.

"If you want me to bring him back, you must let me have a look."

"A look? But you can see... you can see everything!"

"I'm talking about your tits," said Ernest, as if the fact that

he could see her pussy was of no consequence. "Let me look at those babies." He grabbed one of them and pulled on her nightie to release it. The boob flopped out with its wide swollen nipple. He greedily began to knead it.

"Oh, Mister Ernest..."

"When he was little," said Ernest as he groped away, "Bob was even worse than he is now; he'd fuck anything that moved, even goats. So what you've told me about your daughter doesn't surprise me at all and I think you're right to send her to boarding-school, because he would have knocked her up in the end, and you would have ended up being the grandmother of your husband's kid!"

"That's what I thought as well," admitted Laura naïvely.

She was bouncing around on Ernest's sinewy legs whose hairs were tickling her anus; she had granted him the breast he was kneading. He would tug on her nipple from time to time between his hardened workman's fingers, then he'd resume his kneading. Laura was chiding herself, "And I'm just letting him do it." She knew now that this was no dream; dreams never lasted this long. But what could she do? Her entire body was 'eroticised' as she'd once read in a woman's magazine. Every part of her body was responsive and could feel pleasure, her breasts, her buttocks, her genitals, her throat, everything. She didn't have the strength or the willpower to put a stop to it. She powerlessly watched in the mirror as Ernest's other hand moved towards her crotch.

"No, Mister Ernest, I can see your hand, you know, the other one, the one down below... I don't mind you touching my breasts, but not down below. It's too... too intimate."

"Oh go on, love, I'm just foraging around your bush."

She couldn't help giggling. He was so funny that he disarmed

her. At least, that was her excuse. His fingers had reached the edges of her slit, they were going up and down and it gave her goose pimples. Staring at the mirror, she watched them getting ever nearer to her gaping cunt. Ernest was the third man in her life to touch her pussy. There had been her first husband, and she had to admit that he hadn't shown much interest in it, except to conceive her two children. Then there had been Bob, and now his cousin. Well, she blamed Bob. He'd made her depraved, what with all the things he did to her in front of the telly. Ernest's finger straightened and in the mirror, she saw that it was moving towards her clit. She casually moved forward a little and when she felt his finger against it, she yelped indignantly.

"You touched my clitoris, Mister Ernest, I saw you!"

"You're the one who moved forward!"

"I had... I had your thing against my buttocks."

"Get your tits out," he retorted to change the subject. "Give me a feed."

"But you've already... earlier..." It was still hanging out of her baby-doll nightdress with its big brown stiff teat. She pointed at it in the mirror.

"Both of them," said Ernest hoarsely. "Both of them, and you have to show them to me of your own accord, I don't want to force you. If you want me to bring Bob back, you have to be nice to me."

Laura pouted dejectedly and pulled down her décolletage so that it was under her breasts. She then partly turned round and offered them to Ernest. He leaned forward and sucked on one of them. She felt both touched and turned on, as when Bob suckled her. While he was sucking her nipple, Ernest lifted one of her legs.

"Show me your pussy in the mirror now."

Gasping, she leaned back against him. She contemplated the incredible spectacle before her eyes. Both her boobs were on display, one leg was in the air, and everything was spread open. She could even glimpse the cleft between her buttocks and her anus.

"Oh, Mister Ernest, Mister Ernest..."

He stood up, sat her down on the chair, knelt in front of her and lifted her leg again. With both hands, she grabbed hold of the back of the chair to stop herself tipping over.

"I just want to flick my tongue over it," he begged her, "just the once."

"No, you mustn't! You're crazy! I'm all... er... wet. And Bob, earlier, he... I haven't washed."

"Nothing disgusts me in a pretty woman. Those are natural smells."

He spread her labia open and extended his tongue. She put a hand across her eyes so as not to see anything. There she was, burying her head in the sand again! He stuck out his tongue again, like a lizard catching a fly, and licked her two or three times right in the stickiest part, where it was thick and hot and pungent, making her squeal every time. As a finishing touch, he sucked her clit as if he was eating a live mussel, the sort you open with a knife and when you bite into it, it sprays iodine and salty sea water into your mouth. Laura moaned shamelessly. To facilitate his access to her pussy, she had hooked one leg over his shoulder and was pulling him forward with her calf. His tongue was roaming up and down, she could hear him sucking, slurping and nibbling away.

"Oh my God, stop, I'm going to come in your mouth... stop..."

"You're right, that was just to get you warmed up. Let's really go for it now, is that all right with you?"

"Mister Ernest, you've turned me on so much with your tongue that I've lost the strength to resist you, you naughty man! I'll do whatever you want..."

Her nose twitched with some disgust when they were face to face.

"Your mouth... it smells... it smells of..."

"It smells of pussy, what do you think? Come on, I can't bear it any longer, take that thing off, for fuck's sake!"

She let him rip off her nylon nightie. But when she caught sight of her curvaceous figure in the mirror, she couldn't help trying to cover up her chest and bush. Ernest shook his head; he'd just eaten her out and yet here she was pretending to be a Botticelli Venus!

He took off his shirt and, naked as the day he was born (though slightly hairier), he sat down on the chair and placed her on top of him in that same position. With his foot, he dragged over another chair which he placed sideways in front of them, so as not to block the view in the mirror. Then he pulled her back against him as he lifted one of her thighs.

"Put your tootsie on that chair there, it'll be better."

"But... it's terribly indecent... you can see my whole pussy."

"That's the general idea."

He held her tightly against him, forcing her open and clutching her tits. They sat still, contemplating the scene in the wardrobe mirror. He looked at her and she looked at him looking at her. A drop of moisture dribbled out of her hairy cunt onto the chair. They both laughed.

"How could my prat of a cousin cheat on such a beautiful woman as yourself with that tearaway daughter of yours? I

really don't get it. Look at those beauties..." He lifted her heavy boobs. "And this treasure." He put a finger in her slit. Then he had a better idea. He took her hands and placed them on her groin, just above the hairline.

"Why don't you show it to me yourself?"

She remembered the sessions in front of the TV. He didn't have to spell it out for her. She spread her labia with her fingertips.

"Look at that beauty," said Ernest as he fondled her nipples. "Look how easily it opens up."

"Don't you think my outer labia are too big, Mister Ernest? Too chunky? And what about the inner lips, don't you think they stick out too much?"

"I don't think so, no," said Ernest. "I think your pussy's lovely as it is. I like big pussies where there's loads of weird bits sticking out. I think they're sexier than the ones that look like piggy-bank slots. With yours, I can get really stuck in." His finger roamed around her furrow, meandering around the undulating flesh, running from her anus to her clitoris.

"It drives me wild when anyone touches my pussy like that. You're exactly like Bob, you're doing the same things he does, I can tell you're related. Oh God, yes, yes, touch my clit, my big clit! Yes! Pinch it gently, as you did earlier..."

She sighed and arched her back. They both could see the swollen pink flesh of her vagina, as if she was straining to push it out. She pulled hard with both hands on her labia, revealing a pink chasm. He rolled her clit under his forefinger.

"You like being wanked, don't you? You're just like..." He stopped in time and bit his lip hard. He'd almost said, "like your daughter."

"Like who?"

"Oh, no one. Just a woman I used to know. She was like you. Go on, give me your hole and engulf me. From tumescence to revulsion, let's get this over with..." He'd read this sentence in a book set in Egypt and liked to drop it into the conversation whenever he could, just to sound cultivated.

A docile Laura lifted her bottom. In the mirror, she could see that he was pushing his large cock forward. She gently lowered herself onto him and impaled herself. Christ almighty! He made her bounce up and down on his lap, banging her pussy with his big rod. Bob, his eyes popping, had lifted the bedspread to get a better view, like a villain in a pantomime. He was pounding his meat as hard as he could. Fuck, it was even more of a turn-on to watch that bastard screwing Laura than to screw her himself! He had definitely learned a thing or two today. He'd always considered himself the jealous type, but thanks to his ex-con of a cousin, now he wasn't so sure.

While he bounced her on his knee, penetrating her to the hilt, Ernest teased her clit with his fingertips. "Christ," he thought, "I've managed to fuck the whole family in just one night! Well, I haven't buggered Bob, but that can wait. He isn't my type anyway." Laura let rip and started to scream. She tried to control herself, but she couldn't. The sod was fucking her beautifully and he was wanking her at the same time; it was perfection.

"What do you think of my concerto in pussy minor, eh? With pizzicato on the clit? It's my speciality!"

He tugged on her inner labia and fiddled with her clit; he was making her bounce up and down so hard that her big tits were all over the place. She was drooling with joy and yelling the house down.

"Good God," thought Ernest, "I'll have to give her the works.

In the state she's in, she'll do anything, it's now or never." He stretched out his leg and yanked his toolbag towards him. He leaned over to open it without slowing down and immediately found what he was looking for – a strange-looking contraption made up of a large rubber handle and a rubber tube attached to an enema syringe. Holding it in one hand, he made Laura lift herself off him and moved his cock under her arse.

"Oh, Mister Ernest... oh yes... oh yes..."

"I want to know your body inside out," he said chivalrously, "all your holes, all your nooks and crannies."

"Oh, you're right... Bob often takes me this way, you know. I like it."

"I'm an expert. I did it all the time for seven years. Every night in fact..."

"With the prison nurse?"

He almost burst out laughing. "Yeah, right. She was crazy about me."

Holding onto his arms, Laura positioned her anus right above his penis then let herself down onto it with her full weight, impaling herself with a groan of pleasure.

"I can feel it, I can feel it in my bottom... Oh, I love it so much!"

She moved from side to side to feel it more intensely and pushed herself down hard onto it.

"You'll see now, with this thing that doesn't look like much, you'll experience unsurpassed sensations. You'll be on cloud nine."

She was slightly concerned but let him insert the flexible handle of his device into her vagina. Bob sometimes used dildoes on her when he wanted her to be fucked in both orifices simultaneously (under the bed, he was currently considering very different scenarios, possibly involving a third

party), but it was the first time she had seen such a complicated-looking one.

"Is it a dildo, Mister Ernest? You're even worse than Bob! It's a dildo, isn't it? I'm not as naïve as you think!"

He shoved it deep into her pussy and she sighed with pleasure. She loved having both holes filled until it felt as if she was about to explode.

"It's not exactly a dildo, in fact. I made it myself. In prison, I used it to enlarge the arses of young louts that were too tight. You see, cousin, once it's in, you press on the syringe, like so, and it inflates inside you."

"Oh my God! I can feel it swelling inside, you're right... it's like a balloon... wow, this thing is amazing, totally mind-blowing!"

He squeezed the outer syringe, inflating the handle that was inside her. Her vagina swelled up, her slit opened out from the internal pressure so as to become misshapen and her clitoris was as erect as a cockerel's comb.

When she was stretched to bursting point, Ernest made her bounce up and down again and thanks to the pressure of the syringe which dilated her vagina, he felt as if he was buggering a virgin. Her anus was so tight that he had to force his cock in and out and he was almost in pain. In fact, they both were, but that was what made it so wonderful. When he finally came inside her bowels, Laura had had about a dozen orgasms one after the other. She was as limp and as drained as a floorcloth that's just been wrung out. Exhausted and still panting, dripping with sweat, they collapsed onto the bed for a long time, staring at the ceiling.

"I've never experienced anything like this before," Laura confessed, "not even with Bob."

She yawned lazily. She felt unbelievably happy. She was pooped, knackered, wiped-out even, but her body was in peace. She felt slumber creeping up on her, like when she was little and the sandman had come and gone. She wouldn't need any more sleeping pills tonight. She stretched between her 'cousin's' skinny and hairy arms; it felt strange to be here, totally naked, next to this man whom she barely knew.

"I hope you'll come back and see us often," she suggested. "You'll do things to me... that Bob won't know about."

"Yes, it'll be our little secret. We won't tell him anything."

"You fucked me so well! I still can't get over it. At first, I thought it was a dream because it was so intense. I have to go and sleep now. I'm opening up the shop tomorrow morning. My assistant doesn't come in until the afternoon. And maybe Bob will come back, maybe he's just been for a potter in the garden. It wouldn't be wise to stay with you."

She got up, picked up her nightie and put it back on. Ernest walked her to the door. She puckered her lips and on the threshold they exchanged an innocent kiss which made her blush more than what they had just done.

"Promise me you'll come back?"

"I promise."

And off she tiptoed, so as not to wake the children.

"Laura," he whispered. She turned round, her finger in front of her lips. "Get your tits out and lift up your thing. I want to see your arse, I want to see it all as you walk away. I like to see a woman's buttocks jiggle when she walks."

"Honestly, what are you like!" She mischievously wagged her finger at him, but she did what he asked. She bared her generous breasts, hitched up her baby-doll nightdress and started walking downstairs. Ernest leaned on the bannister

and watched her go. He thought it was hilarious to get her to walk around her own home with a bared arse. She passed her children's bedrooms looking like that and until she was out of his sight. Only then did she straighten her clothes while Ernest went back to his room to speak to his cousin. Bob was sitting on the bed looking a bit miffed.

"I know what you're going to say," said Ernest. "But instead of having a go at me and calling me a traitor, you should be thanking me. Yes, thanks to me, your missus will be racked by remorse tomorrow. She will have forgotten that it was you who started it all."

"You're still a right bastard!"

"Admit that you got off on watching us! And think about it. A woman who's that gifted... You should be turning her into a proper slut and sharing her with your mates. I'm sure you'll have a lot more fun with her now that she's tried another cock."

It was a valid argument and Bob, who was well-versed in amorality, had to hand it to him, despite the fact that he was still upset.

All that remained to do now was for them to go downstairs and end the night with Bébé. The little slut would be sandwiched between them. One in her mouth and one in her arse, since she insisted on staying a virgin. Just to give her a few memories to take with her to boarding-school, where there would be only dykes to take care of her assets.

~~~~~

I know what you're thinking, that this story has come to an abrupt end. But stories have to end somewhere, even if it's

just so that another story can begin. Even if it's always the same story that's being told, under different guises. Porn books are like life: you think it's over when it's only just begun, and when you think it's just beginning, it's already over.

SOME THOUGHTS ON PORNOGRAPHY

There comes a point where the superfluous repetition of the most monotonous act ever invented by a living species – to 'make babies' – can get a bit tedious. To avoid the sense of gloom that pervades pornographers (we are all pornographers when we make love) when faced with such extreme banality, they resort to embellishing and dramatising sex. They introduce suspense and grisly plots. Pornography (in books and in life) is like Punch and Judy. But for grown-ups.

Consider the rites that have to be respected in order to 'possess' the object of your dreams (the woman or the man that you fancy, or that you think you do). All those tricky and ludicrous ceremonials where every detail matters, or else it all fails and collapses like a badly-cooked soufflé because lust is destroyed by laughter. How can one desire what makes us laugh? There is consequently nothing more deadly 'serious' than 'fantasy'.

One can't live out one's fantasies with impunity and worse still, one can't make a living from one's fantasies with impunity. For us pornographers, our fantasies are our livelihood and they condition us. By dint of practising this profession, we become what we write about. We become 'twisted'. All the good pornographers that I've met are a bit loopy. As soon as you write a smutty book, your life changes. Writing pornography makes you a pornographer, whether you like it or not and, as the wits would quip, there's no smoke without a fire. These peccadilloes that you recount to turn on your fellow man leave

an indelible stain. Your genitals dissolve in a fog of words; what was possible becomes diluted and impossible. You thought, on the contrary, that you could realise the impossible and live your dreams and daydreams. Pornographers are outside their bodies; their bodies and their souls are quite separate and can only merge through words. The pornographer's words have deadly powers. The freedom of speech of love no longer exists in their wake. Each word that is uttered during lovemaking arouses the ironic echo of what has already been said, it repeats and mimes a past that it reconstructs in order to escape it. It is an absurd challenge.

Like the rest of us, pornographers are alone and their solitude is called sex.

LITERATURE AND PORNOGRAPHY

I hear a lot of drivel about pornography. And about literature. Why on earth should they always be considered opposites? Why do we have, on the one hand, the cream of the literary establishment classed as 'erotic writers' and, on the other, X-rated books? Can literature ever be the fruit of pornography? Or escape it? Or transform it without betraying it?

Is it possible to juggle the two things at once, to back both horses? Ever since I started writing pornography, I haven't ceased to be amazed. What if it was all to do with labels? What if readers were simply judging books by their covers? One would merely have to write on the cover of the most depraved porn book, 'this is not a pipe', sorry I meant, 'this is not porn, it's a real erotic novel', and Bob's your uncle! No, but seriously, how can we cross this invisible boundary between a pornographic

piece of writing and a literary text? At what point does a text become literature? Is it merely a question of polishing one's style, watering down one's wine, beating about the bush and skirting round the act? Are clumsy indulgence and pernickety repetitive description, which are key features of pornographic writing, forbidden in literature? Can pornographers escape the hell of the top shelf or the cellophane-wrapped prison of butchers' stalls-cum-sex shops? Do they have to write 'asexual' books to be accepted in the libraries of gentlemen of breeding?

Why on earth should pornography be the poor relation of proper books? There are good thrillers, good sci-fi novels, so why shouldn't there be good porn novels? Why should the writing of pornography be left to second-rate writers devoid of talent? Why should it end up in the dustbin of literature, in sex shops? What those books have in common is a flatness of style and a lack of imagination; they are merely formulaic consumables (they may even be written following recipe cards, as Donald E. Westlake writes so amusingly in *Adios Sheherazade*), produced by writers incapable of writing anything else.

Unfortunately, porn books are too often a last resort for those writers without talent, failed and embittered writers full of contempt for their readership and for their job, which they consider to be merely a pot-boiler, dismissing it with laughable superiority as 'crap, but it'll tide me over while I look for something better, and it's good enough for those pathetic wankers'. They write novels as if they were Kleenex, destined to be thrown away after use.

The writing that I advocate is the opposite of the *porn* style, but also of the *literary* style. It's a negation of anything

convoluted or excessive, of any sort of expressionist overload, of irony, humour or slap-and-tickle, which simply evade the issue. Metaphors are forbidden, adjectives must be concrete, descriptions should be meticulous without being dragged out. My aim is to achieve transparency of style, thus demolishing any barriers between the reader, who is reduced to the state of voyeur, and the described scenes. Through a form of stylistic asceticism, the author must stay in the background as much as possible, he must stay invisible and must never allow himself the slightest flourish which would draw his existence to the reader's attention. He should strive for the 'degree zero' of writing championed by Roland Barthes for two reasons: so as not to distract the voyeur and so as to eliminate something that becomes rapidly dated: style.

The description of sex should be stripped of the ridiculous and deadly excesses of sex-shop 'pornography' or X-rated videos, as well as the way it has been diverted by tasteful eroticism, that is to say the refusal to show sex as it really is and replacing it with a toned-down and mannered version that is as soluble in writing as instant coffee, a pale imitation of sex whose more or less avowed aim is to substitute pure fantasy with a fairy-tale vision.

The fact is that we're afraid of sex. It may well be ubiquitous, but that sort of sex is watered down, ossified and distorted; it is replacement sex made of rubber. Real sex, with its glitches, its fears, its occasionally unpleasant smells, its grotesque rites, the kind that is practised in real life and not in farcical videos or in fashionable novels about wild young women or ageing swingers who are content only with verbal diarrhoea, that is my Holy Grail.

Is pornography a sexually transmitted disease? Can we

catch it like Aids or the pox? Once we have experienced the pornographic way of making love, that we have resorted to the tricks of pornography, can we ever be cured? Can we ever *become normal again*? Or are we doomed to fall ever further into the depths of sex? What is this pornography that I keep hearing about?

But what if there were two types of pornography? The ubiquitous one that can be found in porn cinemas, sex shops, those pathetic swingers' clubs, Minitel orgies and all kinds of 'fast-sex' ("Hi darling, do you have a credit card? What would you like to talk about?"). And the other pornography. The real one. The pure one. The one that's disturbing and dark. Pornography of the soul? Is sex ill? Is the soul ill? Writing certainly is. Literature is ill.

Or is it an attitude to life? A way of pretending, the way children play at pretending. (Pretending that sex isn't dead boring, pretending it's as exciting as it is in porn). Think about it! 'Pretending' is also what one calls 'literature'. 'An improvement on life' as Charles Bukowski said about fiction. Literature is not life, not as we know it. It's a pretend life. Creating literature with one's genitals, maybe that's pornography?

It entails embellishing the gloomy dullness of 'glandular' sex and replacing it with something more amusing and interesting; being fetishistic about words; dreaming about sex and living this dream as it's happening; overlaying the sexual act with its representation and feeling turned on by this image, by this enactment which is its double (as Clément Rosset would say); being unable to reach what one already has except through fantasy. It's an exhausting exercise. Pornographers are daydreamers who treacherously try to suck you into

their dreams.

I say treacherously because pornography is below the belt. Books that target the reader's genitals are sexual acts. But perhaps sexual acts are already steeped in fiction? Are they not already fictional? When all is said and done, pornography is a tautology.

Is pornography shameful?

Finally, I want to say a few words about *shame*. I'm not ashamed of being a pornographer. I don't consider it a shameful profession. And yet, in a way, because we live in a Judaeo-Christian society, *shame* is my business. Shame is a shady area, it is often used in my novels as a key ingredient to *sexual pleasures*.

Indeed, I believe that without a modicum of shame, sex would rapidly become a dull series of somersaults practised as part of the collective gymnastics of sexual liberation. Sex should never be 'liberated'! Nothing is more tedious than those hardened swingers' orgies; to me they're tantamount to a form of castration. Besides, orgies are unbelievably boring. Aragon, in *Irene's Cunt*, compares an orgy to Chartres Cathedral. To be perfectly honest, without the tremors and embarrassment of 'shame', sex seems insipid to me.

In my writing (particularly my juvenilia), girls have a clear propensity to blush, flush and turn crimson; their hands are clammy, they have butterflies in their stomachs, a pounding heart, rolling eyes, legs like jelly; they babble, they stammer, whine and snivel etc. I've got over this fault, which was becoming a habit. There are fewer innocent young things ripe for initiation in my more recent porn books and more

genuine strumpets and cynical and depraved women. Sign of the times: the 'Justines' of this world have given way to the 'Juliettes'.

They're no different to the women in my life. The sex-pots and the goers who are so dear to me may well believe that they are liberated, but they can never be totally free from 'shame'. They have just enough shame to keep sex interesting. For it is shame that gives them pleasure when animal instincts have banished all concerns about dignity. Girls who are totally shameless when they exhibit themselves, when they offer themselves up, when they adopt certain 'ugly' positions which damage their image, are not as enjoyable (because the pleasure is exclusively physical). They themselves only agree to 'play' with me (or my fellow-men) so as to rediscover the distant taste of that shame that accompanied their first sexual experiences. I have great difficulty in 'playing' with those who have never felt any shame. Sex must not lose its shameful aspect if it wants to remain fun. I use the word 'fun' because it is a game above all else. You play at sex, just as you play cards or the trumpet or in a farce.

The notions of 'sex game' or 'sexual performance' (both playful and theatrical) are crucial. It's all about having fun (like children) while staging fictional scenarios. And about treating one's female playmate (both 'plaything' and 'player') as an effigy of herself, a living imitation. She is never totally herself, she is always playing another persona. This can be a dangerous game because if one puts one foot wrong, the whole thing can collapse into silliness.

WHAT STAGE HAVE I REACHED IN PORNOGRAPHY?

I have written about a hundred porn novels. They all revolved around my sexual fantasies. I am first and foremost a voyeur and so I describe those scenes in minute detail. It's not unusual for me to devote a whole page, if not more, to a description of female genitalia (which is something I am very partial to in my fantasies). A typical scenario is of one or more female characters exhibiting themselves more or less of their own free will, with varying degrees of honesty or cynicism to one or more male voyeurs. The female genitals are the object of desire. They are presented to the reader and consumed by the male protagonists (who revel in their tiniest details, sniffing them, masturbating them, always licking them for a long time before moving onto penetration). I admit that this is a bit of a macho fantasy.

I also have a soft spot for drawn-out scene setting where dialogue plays an important role. Words tend to precede gestures. They serve to 'de-moralise' or 'contaminate' the victim. Characters speak before doing. They say what they want, what they are about to do; these words anticipate the action and already have an impact on the innocent girl's flesh. They can be uttered by a man (the token baddie or the joker) but more typically (this is one of my fantasies, but it is also a very common one) by other women. These 'villainesses', these 'depraved' or 'perverted' girls speak to mock-naïve or sly, hypocritical young girls who become their playthings. The sexual episodes develop slowly; desire, with all its frustrations, matters a lot more than its fulfilment which is ineffable by its very nature. I limit myself to describing sexual satisfaction

in just one or two purely descriptive sentences, never metaphorically. I rarely resort to the 'explosions' or 'rivers of lava' favoured by traditional pornographers. When I do use them, it is as comic relief.

My intention was to drag pornography out of a rut. Have I succeeded? Not really, or only partly. Because even the 'quality' pornography that I advocate is becoming gimmicky. Virtually every 'proper writer' these days wants to try their hand at 'pornography'. The word itself no longer seems scary. I don't want to name any names, but writing porn has become terribly fashionable. That way, one can claim to be open-minded.

Yet porn remains conventional. The word has changed, 'pornography' has replaced 'erotica'; the packaging may be different, but it's still the same unrealistic rubbish. It's sex replaced by something that isn't sex. It's like alcohol-free lager: risk-free, tasteless and it won't get you drunk. That's why most contemporary erotic novels bore me to tears.

Finally, I'm often asked to explain how I differ from other pornographers. Above all, in my love of women. Not just their genitals, but their whole being. Women and nothing but women.

Esparbec.

Some more titles available from the EPS:

The Diary of a Sex Fiend   £9.99
Christopher Peachment

If you're a serious subscriber to political correctness, then this book is probably not for you. But if you are a genial, intelligent and well balanced Renaissance man or woman (as most of us are), then you can do no better than to order this book. In return you will receive a vast repository of acerbic wit, sharp wisdom and an astonishing amount of pithy sexual fact written by the Erotic Review's top columnist, Christopher Peachment.

Rogering Molly & other stories   £7.95
Christopher Hart

From the small market towns of mid-Wales to the narrow streets of ancient Babylon, from a lofty Singapore penthouse (with a rooftop pool the size of Surrey) to a woodland shack deep in the forests of Transylvania, the sexual predators are afoot, and... they're hungry. With an extensive cast of wickedly erotic characters, Hart shows himself to be a subtle master of the genre in these 25 lubricious tales.

The Serving Girl   £7.95
R L Mornington

This is the story of Emily who, while studying, takes up the position of housemaid under the autocratic and mysterious 'Sir". Gradually and intense and highly explicit sexual relationship develops between employer and employee. Everything about this liaison, with its overtones of authority and servility, is extraordinary and unexpected.

Painful Pleasures: £19.95
The Erotic Art of Lynn Paula Russell

Paula's drawings are unashamedly erotic and full of the energies and emotions of sex. Her extraordinary imagination and realistic style carry you effortlessly into a realm of fantasy that is as rare as it is wonderful. There is no better guide to this world than the artist herself; by word and image she brings into play her talents and a special insight born of personal experience to show the reader a hidden door to a world of painful pleasures.

Orderline: 0871 7110 134

Email: eros@eroticprints.org

WWW.EROTICPRINTS.ORG

Please contact us for a catalogue